WATER

MICHAL PERRY ALLEN

LCCN #

ISBN # 979-8-9993765-5-8

Previous novels by this author include.

50 Million Reasons.
Hardcover ISBN# 979-8-218-59496-1
Paperback ISBN# 979-8-218-63189-5

The Evil Within Them.
Hardcover ISBN# 979-8-218-64045-3
Paperback ISBN# 979-8-218-71739-1

Broken Sanity.
Hardcover ISBN# 979-8-9993765-0-3
Paperback ISBN# 979-8-9993765-2-7

TABLE OF CONTENTS

Maddison Graves

Looking in the mirror adjusting her black dress while wiping tears from her eyes. Maddison checks her makeup, hoping she does not need to re-apply more after dedicating two hours of her time, readying herself for the family and friends she was about to receive.

A lite knock on the door startles her. A sound she was waiting for and silently wishing would never come. Without verbally accepting the invitation. The door handle slowly turns as the hinges on the old wooden door make a creaking sound as it opens. Without entering, the funeral director announces from behind the slightly open door.

1

WATER

"Miss Graves. It is time to receive your guests."

"I will be out in a minute."

"Yes Miss Graves, I will let everyone know."

Again, the creaking sound of the old dry unoiled hinges sends a shiver into Maddison Grave's body. The final sound she hears is of the latch's distinct click and the room falls silent again.

One more check in the mirror is needed as Maddison Graves turns to leave the private room she had been instructed to use to collect herself before entering the Chapel. The time had arrived to greet family and friends of her late father.

Walking out of the room she reflects on the man that raised her by himself. The one thought runs thru her head. 'He did the best he could for being a man.' Today he will be remembered and laid to rest for his tiresome commitment to ensuring she had a good life, a college education. Today was his day and she was not about to let anyone in that room deny him that recognition.

2

WATER

Head held high. Maddison Graves poised for a moment before walking in. With the grace and precision her father instilled in her throughout the years of her life. The doors were now held open for her by the assistant director.

She steps in.

Her appearance commanded the room as everyone held their words momentarily, creating a silence. The large room was filled with people to pay respects to her father.

Maddison slowed as she panned the room for her fiancé. There he was, in front of the casket, at the front of the line of people, already shaking hands and accepting well wishes on her behalf.

The abrupt silence caught his attention. There was no mistaking the reason for the silence. Maddison Graves had entered the room. Locking onto her eyes as she walked past the masses of people, taking her position next to him.

Embracing each other signaled to the flock of attendees the couple's commitment to one another. Maddison then began the role of accepting the gracious remarks and condolences from each person passing her in line.

WATER

Father Levi of the St Mary Help of Christians church walked up to the podium requesting everyone be seated in order for the service to begin.

Finalizing the eulogy and listening to all of her father's friends and coworkers take to the podium to express personnel heartfelt stories of her father and how he touched their lives in so many different ways. It was difficult to prevent the tears from rolling down her face. The box of tissues Damien held for her was nearly empty by the time all were finished speaking.

During the speeches, Maddison would recall her father telling the same exact stories these people conveyed about him. How he helped them in times of need. When they needed a deal on a new car or their warranty had expired. He somehow had the ability to ensure everyone who purchased a vehicle from his dealership would never leave unhappy and today proved truth to every word of wisdom and advice on how to handle customers over the years. Madison sat quietly thinking as she recalled how her father always had this one quote.

WATER

"One person's trash is another's treasure. But I don't think anyone told the raccoons."

A lite mist of rain began to fall at the gravesite. Everyone gathered around the casket listening to the biblical quotes from Father Levi. Her father would be laid to rest here. Only the large tent held back the moisture from landing on the gathering of people.

More scripture and prayer before the crowd was dispersed. Maddison and Damien extended invitations for everyone to come to her father's house in the Hamptons afterwards to celebrate his life.

Damien holds the umbrella over Maddison's head as they walk to their car. She asks out loud when the two are seated in the car.

"Why does it always have to rain during a funeral?"

5

WATER

Damien has no words for her. His beautiful fiancé silently staring out of the passenger window. He decides it does not warrant a man's explanation at the moment. Reaching down to press the start button, it was time to let her reflect on this moment. Realizing at this juncture his sole job was to drive them to her father's house, not to begin a debate.

{Silence is sometimes louder than the words you never speak}

The house was now full of chatter and laughter. One toast after another as glasses were raised, lowered and drained then refilled with wine, bourbon, and scotch. Maddison looked out from the kitchen to embrace the noise generated by friends, family, and employees who she personally knew since she was a child. They were loyal to her father until the end.

Stepping up behind her was her father's brother and partner of the car dealership they owned together. Embracing her with a gentle hug, Maddison attempted to pull away from his grip. To no avail she listened to him whisper in her ear.

6

"You will be compensated very well for your father's interest in the dealership. We all know you have no interest in the daily operations. I am sure you've read the will. Shoot, I do believe you helped him write it."

Maddison turns out and away from the one arm grip her uncle Carl had around her waist as she turns to look directly at him, eye to eye with her fiery response.

"You are correct uncle Carl. Law school taught me about contracts, but my father and life taught me more about the devious doings of a partnership. I do agree, I have no interest in pursuing or engaging in a partnership with you. You should not underestimate what I know about you."

"Enough for now Maddison. The company attorney's office will be in touch with you for the transfer of funds. Please sign the documents transferring ownership of the dealership and this house to me as soon as possible. Now if I may, I will leave you to enjoy the rest of your evening."

WATER

With most of the guests departed. Damien and Maddison say the final farewells to the remaining couples as they exit the front doors. Damien steps back away from Maddison. He has a concerned look on his face.

"What is the matter my love? I feel you must still be upset at my father's passing, but you do have a serious look of solicitude on your face. Please explain."

"I want to know what your plans are for us. Now that your father has passed as you stand to inherit a considerable sum of money and compensation as spelled out in his will. I have also been informed you are transferring all of your father's assets to your uncle for a hefty wind-fall settlement. You have obviously pre-negotiated without consulting me. I need to know. Are we still getting married in two months as planned?"

Maddison folds her arms across her chest, remaining silent, facially smirking at Damiens' question. Remembering the wisdom of life's lessons her father the car salesperson instilled in her as she grew into a desirable woman.

8

WATER

"A woman should always make a man squirm before answering him."

Leaving her arms crossed Maddison looked down at the floor, tilts her head side to side, avoiding eye contact with Damien, holding her silence.

He shouts out. "Maddison!"

This triggers Maddison. She turns to look directly at Damien. With a fiery tone she responds.

"Who talked to you tonight Damien? Who got into your head, filling it with this vicious attack in an attempt to destroy our relationship? That information contained in the will is in an NDA."

Damien quickly responds with intensity.

"Your uncle Carl. He cornered me after I saw him talking to you. He mentioned, you will now be set for the rest of your life, considering you've already

9

negotiated with him, and you probably will be dumping me very soon.

I need to know Maddison. Is this your plan? I love you with all of my heart and soul. Why would you contemplate concluding our relationship like this? Are you that unsatisfied with me?"

"Yes, Damien."

Before she could finish her statement, Damien began squirming on queue. Turning his body in circles. Raising both arms as he places his hands on his head in a disgusted mannerism. Then replying.

"Is this your answer to five years together? We have sent out invitations to our wedding. Friends and family have made plans and reservations secured to attend. Not to mention all of the money we have spent on scheduling and catering. Shall I continue?"

"Damien, let me finish before you jump to conclusions."

WATER

Their eyes meet in a stare down relevant to a pair of prize fighters beginning a bout. Maddison is feeling Damiens frustration. Her uncle Carl created a monster she needed to conquer. Uncrossing her arms, slowly placing them on her hips, then raised one hand and a finger signaling Damien should remain silent. Giving her a chance to finish her response.

"Listen to me Damien. Yes, I am indeed getting a settlement for the partnership. I have decided to divest my interest from what I am inheriting. I have no interest in partnering with my uncle or keeping this house my father built. My mother passed away in here shortly after giving birth to me. That memory alone warrants this decision. So, please understand why, I have no interest in keeping it. I thought we discussed this already."

"We have, albeit briefly. Is this your response? Because I am still waiting for the answer to the biggest part of my questioning."

WATER

Maddison presents a big smile and runs into Damiens arms proclaiming her commitment to their union.

"My decision to liquidate the assets I have acquired as of the passing of my father will never come between you and me.

I made this decision for the both of us. We do not need the stress or the connection to my uncle and his destructive mannerism. His demeanor would eventually destroy our marriage. So, to answer your question, yes my love we are still getting married, and we will begin our journey together. I cannot wait to find our dream home to start our own family."

"Maddison!"

"What? Damien."

"Don't scare me like that again. That, last statement? Does that mean you are open to having children?"

"Damien Steale, you better grow a set if you still want to marry me. Don't take everything so personal, you know how I like to tease you. My father created and shaped my personality. This is what you are getting. Take it or leave it. To answer your question. Having your child will show you how much I love you. Even if it kills me as it did my mother."

"I will take it. All of it. All of what you have to offer. As for your mother, that was the doctor's fault, nothing hereditary. You know that."

"Do we have a deal Maddison?"

"Yes Damien, we have a deal. Now roll up those sleaves big boy we have some cleaning up to do."

"What? Where are the housekeepers?"

"I can put that uniform on later for you if you will pitch in and help?"

"DEAL!!!"

13

{Next day. 10:00AM

Corporate lawyers' office.}

"Thank you Maddison for coming in today. I have everything prepared for you to sign. It has been prepared as you instructed. One large initial installment and yearly payments to be deposited into your account. I've have included the nondisclosure agreement along with the breach of contract clause you requested. It is as airtight as I can make it, within the law."

"Have the employees mentioned anything? Any mutinies on the horizon?"

"Nothing has come up. Everyone wants and needs their position at the company. I will note, it may be a matter of

14

time. Especially when they find out Carl is now at the helm and not you. They really were expecting you to take over the company."

"Sorry to disappoint them, not my problem anymore. Although I must ask. You have not mentioned the failure to continue operations amendment."

"Page 42, I buried it in the fine print with fancy language he will never understand the wording until it's necessity to implement. You and I know your uncle Carl will try something underhanded as soon as he can figure out a scheme."

"Perfect, excellent work. Now, where do I sign? Damien and I are going house hunting after this."

"Good to hear you two are moving forward. You need a threshold for him to carry you over. Are you planning on children?"

"Maybe one day. It is the only thing I hold in reserve about getting married. You know about my mother passing after giving birth to me. Having children would be mentally challenging to me. But, who knows what the future will bring."

WATER

"I understand Maddison. Good luck to both of you on that note."

The final signature now penned to the sixty-page document. Maddison stands up shakes her lawyer's hand and without another word, exits the office to her car where Damien is waiting.

He asks.

"All done?"

"Yes"

"Any regrets?'

Maddison turns to him and locking on to his eyes for what seemed an eternity. Then gently responds.

"Hell No! Now drive us away from here."

WATER

"OK then, Where Too?'

"Anywhere, let's go to the countryside for a road trip. I need time to collect my thoughts."

"Got it."

The engine cranks with a roar from the exhaust. The 305 V8 chevy small block sends a vibrant sound the whole city block recognizes. It was her daddy's 1979 cherry red, El Camino. The only item written into her contract that she wanted to keep. Her daddy promised it would be hers one day and she demanded he keep his word to the day he passed away. Damien pressed on the accelerator steering the car down the highway like it had just been sold off the dealership lot.

Maddison's father meticulously maintained it and kept it in the showroom at the dealership on full display for every customer to salivate and dream about as they awaited their own car deals to complete. Many wealthy customers offered enormous funds trying to acquire it.

Each time they did they were met with the same answer.

"It is my daughter's car and is not for sale."

"STOP DAMIEN! STOP THE CAR."

"Maddison what happened?"

"Turn around, That is it, that's the house I am looking for."

"What?"

"Just turn around please."

Damien makes a safe U-turn and proceeds back the way he was driving.

WATER

"There, right there. Park here. Do you see it? That is the house I have been dreaming of and wanting my whole life."

"Maddison, you are kidding me, wait is this another one of your ways to tease me. Am I somehow being tested before our union?"

"Silly man, get out of the car and let's go meet that lady on the porch. She just put the for-sale sign by owner out in the front yard."

Damien hesitated too long before exiting the El- Camino when Maddison turns around pacing a few steps back to the car, bending over to look in thru the passenger window, she voices her command.

"Get OUT of the CAR!"

Shocked and dismayed, like a young pup not fully potty trained. Damien turns off the ignition and exits the car, following behind Madison's pace. She arrives at the foot of the steps to the porch moments before him.

WATER

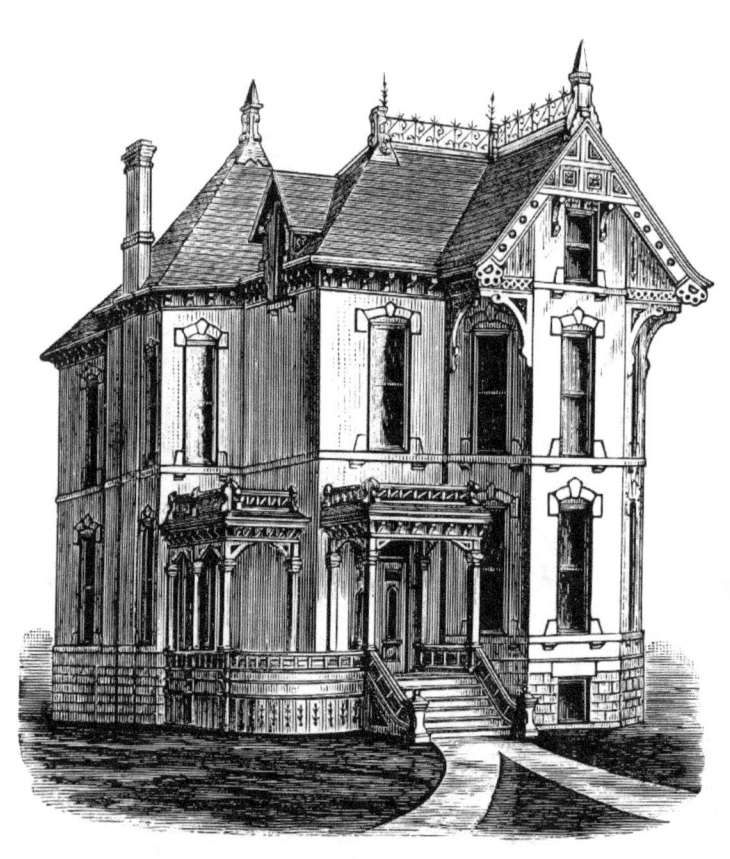

The House

Standing on the porch clutching her cane, the elderly lady turns to see Maddison approaching her from the steps behind her. Hold up her cane in a defensive posture. She yells out at the unknown young woman. She yells out.

"WHO ARE YOU? WHAT DO YOU WANT? I DON'T HAVE ANY MONEY."

"Madam, I am deeply sorry for startling you. My fiancée and I were driving by, I saw you placing the for-sale sign in the front yard. We turned around and I am inquiring about your house.

22

"Oh! yes, I have decided it needs to be sold. It was my father's home and my grandfathers before him. He has finally passed away. Are you interested?"

"Absolutely, may I introduce myself. I am Maddison Graves, and this gentleman is my fiancé Damien Steale. What can you tell me about the house, and can we look inside?"

"Nice to meet you Madison and your fiancé. What did you say this handsome man's name was?"

"I am Damien Steele."

Extending his hand towards the homeowner. She places her hand on his. He could feel it was not the hand of a frail older woman. Even though she walked with a cane, her hand felt young like Maddison's. Her skin was much softer, and her grip was strangely stronger than he had anticipated for the age of the woman he was introducing himself too.

Maddison interrupts the exchange with her question.

WATER

"I am sorry, we did not get your name."

Still holding Damien's hand and looking into his eyes with hers. She replies to Maddison without turning her head to acknowledge her. Damien is now uneasy with the situation he is encountering as the woman finally releases her grip and eye contact to answer Maddison.

"My manners, where have they gone all these years. Please accept my apology, I am Annette Lancefield. My grandfather built this house in 1891. I am sorry but I do not have time to show you around today. I was just up here locking the door when you came up behind me. Although I will be back in town at the start of next week. I will be traveling to Miami, Florida to meet with some friends. Here is my card with my contact information on it.

24

I can meet you here and show it to you. If you are still interested by then. You are welcome to look around outside and the grounds of the property until then."

"Thank you Miss Lancefield, I will give you a call next week and yes if you don't mind we will walk the property to get a feel for it. Do you need some help navigating the steps and to your car?"

"Young lady, I only have this cane in my hand for self-defense, I am perfectly capable of walking down those steps and to my car."

Maddison and Damien watch as Annette swiftly exits down the steps with the ease of a younger woman, picking up her stride as she continues along the stone walkway leading away from the house.

Halfway before Annette reaches the mailbox, she stops to turn back towards them addressing the couple she left speechless, on the porch with a parting thought.

"Remind me to tell you about the water faucet down in the basement and that dam mailbox when we meet again. Without hesitation Annette returns to regain her stride down the walkway, carefully navigating the stones.

Instead of continuing on her otherwise straight path to reach her car she strays away from the walkway to take an alternative course that takes her across the grassy lawn instead of towards the mailbox, mumbling under her breath."

"I hate that mailbox."

Maddison and Damien are speechless, standing on the porch watching her place the cane in the back seat and drive away. Turning to look at each other with dismay. Damien asks the first question.

"What is with the water faucet?"

Maddison replies.

"What's with the Mailbox? She avoided that thing like it was cursed."

"Madison, I think we should pass on this house."

WATER

"Damien, This gives me more incentive to look into buying this house. It may have some history and talking points when we have quests over for dinner."

"If it makes you happy, Although I believe you should take a look at the exterior and interior of the house before you commit. Don't forget she needs to tell us about the water faucet. That gives me concern Maddison."

"I agree with you Damien, let's go look around before deciding. Before we leave, I want to walk over to the mailbox."

{Two weeks later.}

It is Sunday morning on Long Island, NY. The aroma of freshly brewed coffee fills the house awakening Maddison. Damien must be here she assumes. He always comes over on Sunday for the coffee and to make her breakfast. Rising from her slumber, Maddison reaches for her robe to join her companion downstairs in the kitchen.

"Good morning pretty lady."

"No breakfast for me this morning, I am not feeling it today, just coffee please."

"Have you called that lady about the house.?

"I forgot, now where did I put the card she gave me?"

"You put it in the glove box of the El Camino."

"Be a good boyfriend and retrieve that for me and I will call her when I am finished with coffee."

"Here is your first cup. I will be right back."

"I have no doubt you would jump off a cliff if I asked you too."

"Maddison, I do have a limit to my love for you."

"Um, no you don't."

WATER

Damien decides he will end it there and walks to the garage to retrieve the card from the glove box in the El Camino. Hiding the card in his shirt pocket just before reentering the kitchen he displays a frown on his face to proclaim.

"I looked everywhere in the El Camino; I cannot find it."

"What? It has to be there. I remember placing in there when we were leaving."

Maddison slips off the island chair, quickly marching out to the garage. Robe coming undone and flowing behind her, runs into the garage and around to the car to the passenger door. Opening the door, she releases the lock on the glove box to frantically begin searching thru a pile of papers left in there for years. Quickly she empty's the contents from the compartment. The pile of papers removed and now laid out on the bench seat; she carefully sifts thru them.

Finally giving up her search she exits the vehicle. Standing erect and staring at the papers on the seat one last time. On the other side of the car is Damien taking in the view of a lifetime. There in front of him was his beautiful girlfriend, looking as if she had stuck her finger in an electrical socket. Her normally beautiful hair in disarray and her robe open exposing her breasts to him.

All Damien good do was stand next to the driver's side holding the card up for her to see, with a big smile on his face to say.

"Is this what you are looking for?"

Maddison shouts.

"Damien! You let me go nuts searching for that card and you have been holding it the whole time?"

"Gotcha! And thanks for the memory of you at this moment. I will cherish this forever. If only I had a camera."

Maddison calmy walked around to the driver's side of the car. Leaving her robe open completely exposing her naked body to Damien. She reached for the card with one hand while leaning up to give him a kiss.

But, instead grabbed his man-hood with her free hand and declared.

"Two can play this game boyfriend. Now let's go finish our coffee."

Dialing Annette.

"Misses Lancefield, this is Maddison Graves. Do you remember me? We met you at your house the day you were placing the for-sale sign in the yard."

"Yes, Maddison. I remember you. Would you like to see the house now?"

"Indeed, I am, when can we schedule a time to view it?"

"I will be there after lunch today, let's say, one O'clock, does that suit you?

"Damien and I, will be there and thank you for showing us your home."

Madison ends her call with Annette. Damien is finishing the kitchen duties of cleaning up after his breakfast. She reports to Damien that her conversation was a pleasant one and requests he drive her to the house to meet her at one O'clock.

"Maddison, you know I planned to play a round of golf today with my boys from college. This is the last Sunday of the month. You know I have a standing tee time the Last Sunday of every month."

"I think you should make a sound decision to accompany me to visit with Annette. If you need more convincing I will be in my room."

With that said. Maddison turned to walk away from the kitchen Island. While turning away she drops her robe on the

32

floor. Walking away naked up the stairs to her bedroom.

Damien was left speechless. Standing at the edge of the kitchen Island, he watches Maddison walk away and up the stairs. Unable to take his eyes off of her.

Looking down at the robe on the floor, then he turns his head to glance at his golf clubs resting beside the front door, then back at the robe on the floor. It was decision time.

At that moment he knew who was going to be the one wearing the pants in the relationship. Without hesitation, Damien bent over to pick up the robe and followed Maddison up the stairs.

{1:00PM The house showing begins.}

The, El Caminos' brakes begin slowing the car to a stop in front of the house. Maddison looks out the passenger window to see Annette has already arrived and is sitting in a rocker under the portico. Exiting the vehicle, she looks back to see

WATER

Damien has learned his lesson and is already out of the car flanking her left side. A gentle smile is formed with her lips, With her man by her side she lovingly grasps his arm to walk with him to the base of the steps.

"Good afternoon lovebirds. Step up here and have a seat next to me my dear. You there, young man can excuse yourself to venture inside to look around. Take care to step into the basement where you will find two sets of faucets. I will explain them to you after Maddison, and I have a chat. We will meet you inside soon enough. Off you go now."

After a wave of Annette's hand to hurry Damien along. Maddison gave Damien a look with a stern face. He knew this was his queue to obey the woman's command as he then excuses himself to walk inside.

"Now that it is us girls left to chat. What would you like to know about the house?"

WATER

"Of course, I have a few questions for you."

"Before you start babbling out a lot of questions, Let me begin with who actually lived here. You see, My grandfather built this home in 1881 for him and my grandmother. After they passed my mother and father inherited it. Now it is left to me, and I do not want anything to do with it. Now, you may ask your questions."

"How old were your grandparents when they passed and did the go peacefully in their home here?"

"Peacefully you ask. No, my dear, they were healthy. Never went to a doctor a single day while they were living here."

"Then how did they pass if they were as healthy as you claim?"

"My grandparents drank the water from the faucet in the basement. He claimed it was the water and the sole reason gramps and grandmother maintaining a healthy life together. When my grandfather built the house he noticed some water seeping out of the blockwork in the basement. He was unable to stop it

35

from seeping out so, he jokingly put a faucet over the seepage.

One day he was filling the family pet's water bowl when he discovered he used the wrong faucet. The dog was old and frail. The veterinarian diagnosed her with some odd hip disease. My grandfather being who he was decided to give the poor dog the water. I surmised he was too lazy to empty it and re-fill it with water from the correct faucet."

"So, sad how long did the old dog live beyond that day. That water must have tasted terrible.?"

Annette hesitated for a few seconds to reply.

"That dog was cured in a few days. Old Charlie ran around like a pup for ten more years. After that, my grandfather began drinking the water himself, claiming the water had the power to cure all their illnesses."

"If the water was so powerful, then why are they not here? How did they die?"

"You see that mailbox out there? My grandmother went every day to meet the mail carrier to get the mail. Honestly, she had a thing for him. One day she walked out to meet the mail carrier at the mailbox and slumped over and there she laid. Grandfather was always watching grandmother meet the mail carrier for their daily chat. He saw her fall, then ran out of the house to see what had happened to her and that was it.

The mail carrier found them laying together. He was holding her in his arms when he perished as well, together at the base of the mailbox."

"That is a sad story. I am deeply sorry for you, losing your grandparents that way. Did your parents inherit the house after they passed?"

"Yes, they did. True to the fairy tale my grandfather told us about the water from the faucet. My father decided to try it one day after my mother became ill while carrying me to term."

"Did it work?"

"My father claims it did and continued to use the water which kept them both healthy until they both passed away. Again, they never went to another doctor after they started drinking the water."

WATER

"I am amazed at this story. When did they pass and how did they die if they were healthy and also drinking the water?"

Annette cleared her throat, reliving the loss of her grandparents and her immediate parents was emotionally challenging to convey. Once she had collected her composure she began to finish her story.

"Just as my grandmother once walked to that mailbox, my mother walked the same stone walkway to the mailbox as the scenario of history repeated itself when my father followed her."

"No! Not again!"

"The new mail carrier found them at the base of the mailbox. My father holding my mother in his arms just like his father before him."

Tears were now forming on Annette's cheeks as she ended her family's story. Attempting to wipe them away with her sleeve, Maddison silently offers a tissue from her purse.

"You do not have to continue; I now know the answer to one of the questions I wished to ask of you."

"I am sure you understand Maddison, why I cannot walk psst that mailbox."

"Are you afraid you might perish if you do?"

"Not really. What bothers me the most is I do not have anyone to hold me in their arms and perish with me. So, I cannot let that mailbox claim me alone."

WATER

House Tour

"Miss Lancefield. Are you sure you want to sell this house at this time? You have fond memories to this place. Selling it will close this chapter of your life to a family legacy. You look healthy enough to still live here for many more years. By the way did your father or mother allow you to drink from the faucet?"

"My darling I sense you have some reservations about the water story. I assure you if you want this house, you too will begin to drink from the faucet. Not one person has ever resisted the urge to try it. Since 1881. Every guest that has visited gives it a try. My grandfather would go to church every Sunday. If he received word of a person in need or had an illness, he would invite them here to drink from the faucet."

WATER

"How many people took it as an elixir."

"Oh! Madison, No one thought it was an elixir or some magic potion. But it did cure many of my grandfathers' visitors. At least they claim it cured them. The true believers walked or drove from miles away to ask for a chance to drink from the faucet. My grandfather obliged everyone who would believe him."

"Is there any documented proof or case studies that could concur with the results?"

"Let me enlighten you with some stories that may convince you it helped people. One morning a young lady brought her infant son to our door. He had been burned with hot grease from a deep fat fryer. My father took the child downstairs. Placing the crying child's arm under the faucet so the water could flow over the burn. Immediately the child quit crying. He no longer felt the pain from the injury.

WATER

Next my father wrapped the child's arm in a bandage soaked in the water. The woman tried to pay my father, but he refused. They came back each day for a week. Each time his mother brought him here, my father would remove the bandage to see his arm had improved until one day he did not need the water anymore. He was healed."

Maddison held her thoughts. Thinking the story couldn't be true, water has no power to heal a person. A few moments pass when Maddison asks.

"Please tell me more."

"Come with me Maddison. We will tour the house now and I will show you a wall of pictures my grandfather and father took of the people they claimed to have saved with the water. I know all of the stories behind everyone in the frames. I cannot bear the burden of taking them down. I must leave that to someone else."

WATER

Annette rose from her rocking chair with Maddison following behind, Opening the front door to enter the house then a short walk to the living room. There in the middle of the room was Damien silently staring at the walls of the room.

Maddison stepped up beside him, noticing not one inch of wall was visible. It was no wonder Damien never came back out to sit with them.

Maddison startles her fiancée by walking up to his side, joining him in the long stare, at all of the photographs in front of them. Maddison breaks the silence and whispers to Damien.

"There's hundreds of them, everywhere, in this room, on every wall."

Damien turns to Annette to ask her a pondering question.

"Who are these people, why are these pictures on the walls?"

"They are the saved, the sick, the hurt, the skeptical turned believer, the people who have lost all hope, the

44

desperate, the families, the children of parents that would not give up.

Sisters, brothers, aunts, uncles, friends, religious and atheists, with curable and incurable disease or diagnosed as terminal. These are the people my father and his father, before him, came from everywhere imaginable to drink the "water."

Maddison and Damien stood with their backs touching each other as they slowly turned within their space to view as many pictures as possible in the brief time they stood there.

Maddison broke away from her stare at the pictures to address Annette. Pointing at a pair of photos on the wall. These two photos' next to each other. It looks like the same gentleman in both photos."

"You are correct. He came to my grandfather from the southern state of Mississippi. The first picture is of him with a spinal problem from birth. Calcium build-up, known as arthritis, to most. As with everyone on these walls, he heard about the water and found his way here. Within a month of drinking the water he

45

could stand tall instead of being hunched over in pain for years. He left his cane here, as a gift to my grandfather. That is, it over against the wall there."

Annette pointing to a corner of the room at a single hand carved cane leaning against the wall. Maddison turned to look at Damien.

"Damien, did you find the faucet in the basement?"

"Yes, I saw two down there, one attached to a network of piping, the other attached only to the stone wall. What is that about? Please tell me why this room is full of pictures?"

"Pick out a picture Damien." Said Maddison.

"What, Why?"

"Just pick one!!!"

WATER

"OK, this part of the wall is filled with children. The skinny one here. She doesn't look healthy. What happened to her and why am I seeing pictures of children in this house?"

Maddison replies.

"Damien, I will fill you in later. Annette can you tell us the story behind this child? Please."

"Her name is "Serenity." Her parents named her after a tornado had passed near her parents' house. The noise during the storm was so loud the parents were sure they were going to perish. Once it moved on from the area it became silent with a surreal feeling. As soon as they were able, the parents ventured outside of the bunker to view the devastation. Shortly after that the mother went into labor and "Serinity" was born.

She developed a rare blood disease. I cannot recall the name of the diagnosis; I was a child at the time and did not understand a lot of what my parents were doing with the water. Apparently the team of doctors gave up trying to cure her with powerful drugs when they informed her parents none of the drugs they prescribed had any effect and no cure was available.

At the advice of a holistic medicine practitioner and once again it was word of mouth and desperation that her parents brought her here to try the water.

The parents were losing hope when every option available to them failed to provide a cure for their daughter. They boarded a train travelling from Kentucky to meet my father, begging him to let her stay here in my room with me until she was well enough to go home. This place was their last hope.

When she returned to Kentucky completely cured of her disease her parents took her back to the same physicians. Denying the results they declared her healthy outcome an anomaly and would not confirm it was the water when the parents provided them with the information and evidence of the action they embarked on.

Obviously taking matters into your own hands is not in a physician's best interest. They get their egos hurt."

WATER

"Annette, I would love to hear more stories, but for now can we tour the rest of the house?"

"Of course, let me show you the kitchen. When my father took over the house he upgraded the kitchen from a wood burning stove to a modern electric one. My grandparents used an old ice box for a fridge. A guy in a truck came by every other day to sell them a block of ice. I used to get in trouble when we visited in the summer because I would stick my head in there to cool off.

My father and mother upgraded the electric service and added electrical appliances when we moved in. The wood stove heated the kitchen up to an unbearable temperature. Thus, my reasoning for occasionally putting my head in the ice box.

Would you like to see the bedrooms?"

"Yes we would."

Damien excuses himself once again.

WATER

"Maddison you can look at them with Annette. I want to look into the source of the water faucet downstairs again. Is there a source, like a well that feeds the magical faucet Annette?"

"As long as you call it magical and remain skeptical. No water will come out. There are no sources or pipes running to it. At least that is what my grandfather told all of us. It comes out of the wall. If a skeptic stands in front of it, it will not produce water."

Damien looks at his fiancé with a serious look of skepticism, then slowly turns away from the two of them while remarking.

"Maddison, I will be off exploring. Let me know when you are ready to leave."

"Yes of course my love."

Once Damien is out of sight Maddison turns to speak to Annette.

WATER

"Shall we continue to the bedrooms Annette?"

"Right this way."

Stepping away from the picture room, Annette leads Maddison thru a doorway to a large bedroom. Inside there is a queen size colonial post bed, complete with mosquito netting draping from the posts. The floors crackled under foot as if they were in pain from being abused.

Maddison stood idle at the center of the room. Looking at the windows and the twelve foot ceilings. The architectural crown molding is still intact, albeit the paint had begun to fade and peel off in places.

Walking over to the windows she opens the drapes to allow light to shine into the dreary darkened interior. As with older designed homes, she noticed the windows lined up from one side of the room to the other. Obviously to capture a cool nightly cross breeze thru the room.

Mesmerized by the beauty of the old home she drifted back in time to experience the timeline when Annette broke into her dream.

WATER

"This is the main bedroom. As you can see it is quite large. My grandfather grew up in a small cabin in the woods. When he built this house he demanded it have a large bedroom for him and Grandmother. It has this chase lounge against the wall here next to the window. Grandfather always joked that he needed that for when he was in the doghouse.

The Bathroom is quite large as well with a separate room for the dirty business. Back then the plumbing always backed up, so, it had a door of its own."

Following her assignment as a tour guide. Annette led her into the bathroom.

"I love this antique bathtub. It looks new, like it was never used."

"Now, you have a good picture of my grandparents. I do not know how the two of them slept together, all those years. Especially without modern air conditioning."

"What about your room. Can I see it now?"

"Yes, follow me. It is on the other side of the house."

"Lead the way."

The old structure was not only built with windows lining up. It also had the doorways lining up with the windows. Although Maddison feared the windows would need replacement and figuring they would be swollen shut and not able to open them.

"This room is smaller than the other bedroom. Although my grandfather did install its own bathroom similar to theirs. He wasn't much of an interior designer. So, he left the décor up to grandmother. She did her best to give this old shack a female's touch."

"I can see that with the drapes and linens. I'm guessing, the house has been closed up for some time."

"Yes, I too can smell the musky aroma. It needs some tender loving care. And maintenance. I am getting too old myself and I really do not care to pump money into it."

"Annette. Can we go back into the picture room; I would like to hear one more story before we leave."

"Of course, my dear. Walk thru that door and you will be back in there. This house is built in a circular pattern for getting around in it."

The two have now arrived back in the picture room to see Damien once again staring in awe at the enormous amount of photos on the wall when Maddison asks.

"Have you finished exploring the place? Did you find the source of the water for the faucet?"

Turning to face the two women. Damien exposes his facial expression as a deer in the headlights and finally responds to Maddison's question.

"I found two faucets down there. Not far apart from one another. I had an experience unlike any I have encountered in my life before this day.

54

WATER

Maddison, I have a lot of questions, and I also have concerns that all these people in these photographs may have been duped into believing they were drinking magical water from one of those faucets down there. That it would somehow cure them when a doctor could not."

"So, Damien, does this mean you are skeptical of what Annette is telling us?"

"Yes, Maddison and I think you should be skeptical as well. We will discuss this privately later at home, I will be outside waiting on you in the car."

Madisson stood her ground while watching Damien storm out of the house. Failing to acknowledge Annette in his haste to retreat.

Maddison remains calm as she walks slowly around the room looking at the photos. Stopping occasionally to stare at a photo. It was an eye-to-eye personal connection to the person in the photo looking out at Maddison looking in.

Annette sensed she was intrigued to know all of the stories and not just a few. Breaking in again to Maddison's thoughts.

WATER

"If you need to go with your Fiancée we can discuss this later."

Finally stopping in front of a photo, Annette knew she was ready, when Madison pointed her finger and said.

"This one. Tell me about this lady. She looks familiar. And pregnant."

"Her name is Darlene. She is from Ohio. Came down here with her husband. Stayed in the local bed and breakfast for six months. They had been trying to conceive a baby. Doctors could not figure out why she could not bear children. Every test and exam they ordered on both her and her husband were normal. Again, they were stumped and left them with no options to consider.

When they heard about the water, they packed up and drove into town looking for my father. Of course, he was happy to oblige and let them come here daily to drink the water. Then they would go back to the bed and breakfast to try again. I suppose they had a lot of fun giving it a go every day."

56

WATER

"I bet they did." Said Maddison.

"That picture was sent to my father after she was four months along."

Maddison looked at the picture again and then back to Annette to ask.

"Did the water help them conceive that baby?"

"All I will say is, the thank you note that came with the photo, said the baby was eight pounds, seven ounces at birth."

Maddison had a tear in her eyes as she looked back at the photo. Annette could see Maddison was moved by the story and asked why the story caused her to be emotional.

"My own mother died from complications giving birth to me."

"I am so sorry. Maybe you should go now. I am sure the man out there needs to go home and talk to you about his experience with the faucet. Let me know when you would like to return. I will tell you more stories of the house."

WATER

"You are right, He's probably in a mood right now. I will contact you next week to re-schedule a visit."

"Goodbye for now, Maddison."

Leaving the house, Maddison walks down the stone walkway towards the mailbox but stops a few steps away from it to give it a stare, then decides to veer around it, taking an alternate path down the lawn to the awaiting El Camino.

WATER

WATER

Seriously

Maddison joins Damien in the vintage Chevrolet El Camino. The engine restarted, warmed up and idling. Realizing her prince charming had already decided he is not opening the door for her, she lets herself in and sits down in the passenger side of the bench seat. Remaining next to the door instead of sliding next to her man. Since he did not open her door, he does not get a snuggle.

Placing the gear shift in drive, Damien pulls away from the house. The drive home is sultry and dry. Neither speaks a word of the time they have spent in the house.

Damien reaches up to the visor to press the garage door opener. Pulling in, he shuts off the engine. Neither of them makes the first move to get out of the car when Damien reaches for the button once again to close the door behind them. Still no movement from Maddison or Damien. She is staring straight ahead thru the windshield.

Then:

Maddison asks.

"Are you going to be a gentleman and open my car door for me, or do I have to do this myself?"

Damien calmly turns his head towards his bride to be. She holds steady refusing to look at or acknowledge him. Savoring the moment, he lets her fume a few seconds before reaching for his door handle to open the driver's door.

Now stepping out, he begins a slow walk to Maddison's side of the car. Flipping the keys in a circular motion on his fingers as he walks in front of the car. Still no eye contact or acknowledgement. Reaching her side of the car he places the keys in his front pocket then reaches down to open his princess's door.

WATER

Stepping out to stand up, she is now face to face with Damien.

Damien reaches out with his arms for her waist and pulls her in close for a hug and a kiss.

Maddison melts in his arms, then replies.

"Are those keys in your pocket or are you happy to be holding me close to you?"

"You know how your spats turn me on."

"SERIOUSLY? My spats. Don't get me started. Let's discuss in the house."

"SERIOUSLY? We are not…."

Maddison is released from Damiens' arms and walks in the house from the garage while saying.

"Nope, rain check. Later tonight, maybe. I want to discuss the house and what exactly did you find out about the faucets downstair in the basement and what did you experience?"

Standing by the car at a loss for words. He pulls the keys from his pocket and places them on the hook by the door, then hits the light switch and follows Maddison in the house.

Maddison sits at the kitchen's island bar then requests Damien to prepare a snack while they discuss the house. Damien reaches in the refrigerator for the deviled eggs previously prepared earlier and sets them in front of her.

"You are amazing boyfriend. I love how you think ahead."

"Ok, What do you want to know?"

"Where does this mysterious water come from?"

"I am not sure. It seems the faucet is bolted to the wall, but I cannot confirm any piping is attached to it unless I remove it from the wall. The other faucet's piping is exposed, and you can follow its connection to other piping. You cannot do that with the magical one. I do not think I can figure out the source until it is removed from the wall, and we cannot do that unless we or you buy the house.

"Small details Damien that will be in the prenup agreement."

"A prenup, SERIOUSLY! Maddison."

"You are so gullible Damien. I would never do that to you."

"If you do decide to purchase the house, are you willing to drink the water from that faucet? And what if someone comes up to the house and asks for a drink? Are you willing to accept the traffic we might encounter? I saw those pictures, you saw the people in those pictures. What was your take on them?"

"Number one my darling I am not sick and have no reason to drink the water as for number two, we will both have to make that decision if we buy it."

WATER

"Wow, you said 'WE' So, I get a vote in this decision? Are you softening up my hard nose lover?"

"From my viewpoint the only thing hard is what's in your pants."

"Obvious huh?"

"Wait, you put a cucumber in your pants when I was not looking, didn't you?"

"Obvious, HUH!"

"Remind me not to eat a salad at dinner tonight."

"Deal."

"I do have a serious question Hon. What do you make of all those photos and the stories she has behind each one? Those people actually showed up and claimed to have been healed by the water."

"Maddison, I am not convinced each of those photos are real, as for the stories, I have the same opinion. I went downstairs and looked at that faucet, turning it on, nothing came out. But the vibe I got from touching it scared the crap out of me. I thought I was getting electrocuted."

"What? An electrical shock?"

"Yea, strange huh?"

"Yes, Shocking?"

"You think that is funny don't you?"

"Of course not, but she did mention if you were a skeptic it would not provide water to you."

"I will admit this Maddison; I am suspicious of the activity she claims to know about. She may be misleading you for the sake of selling the house above market value. Have you spoken to her about the selling price?"

"Not yet, Although you may have a point. Ask yourself, how would she be able to fake all of those pictures and quote the many different stories associated with each one of them, with such great detail?"

"I see we have more questions than answers. I am getting hungry for dinner. You want a salad?"

"SERIOUSLY DAMIEN?"

WATER

"You think I am being funny?"

"Give me a break, Damien."

"One more point of interest Maddison. If this 'water' does have holistic, mystical, magical power that we could prove exists beyond a doubt. It would be a scientific breakthrough for the medical community."

"Damien, think about how the nay sayers in this town would make a mockery of us. There is no absolute clinical proof that the water heals anyone of any disease or a medical problem any person in those photos believes they had.

I will finish with this. If all of this were true. That family should have profited on its ability to heal. Instead, they kept it a sweet little secret for over a hundred years."

"Maddison, there are people all over this earth that believe in healing springs. They exist all over the world. I know of one healing spring in South Carolina where people travel to it each summer to swim in it.

WATER

Think of the money we can make by marketing this to a specific group of people. The sick and dying need hope when all else has failed them."

"Damien, they never marketed it for the monetary value it could bring them. They simply believed it would cure illnesses and save their lives. They had faith in the water's ability to heal.

'FAITH' Damien. It was their FAITH.'

That is all those people had and all they needed was their faith and belief that the water was the answer to their condition."

It was at that moment the kitchen grew colder than normal for the warm spring air circulating in from the open windows. Maddison was chilled and needed a sweater. Putting Damien in his place at that moment, sent her fleeing upstairs to her closet. Walking up the stairs she shouted back at him.

WATER

"I will be back down in a minute. Are you not cold?"

"No, I am fine, maybe you need some water. For medicinal purposes only"

"Shut up, Damien, that which is not funny."

Moments later Maddison returns to the kitchen. Damien has begun preparing dinner for the two of them. Hearing her footsteps as she exited the last step of the stairs. Damien turns away from the flat top to gaze at his beautiful fiancé. No sweater, she is wearing a thin blouse minus a bra as usual.

"Back to your old self, No sweater needed?"

"Funny thing is when I reached my closet, I had a hot flash. I am nowhere close to menopause so, I do not recommend a smart-ass remark about it."

"I would NEVER!"

"Yea, right. What are you preparing for us tonight chef? I do appreciate your love of cooking. You will make a good wife someday."

"Gump style shrimp in a creole sauce."

"Oh nice, can you run for me also?"

"Now look who's making smart-Ass comments. Joking aside, I also made bruschetta for an appetizer. Let me ask you a few more questions."

"Fire away captain."

"If you buy the house. Are you planning to renovate it and take down all those pictures?"

"That is a hard question to answer at the moment. I like the history the place has to offer. Although I could not live there with all of them staring out from the photos."

"You could continue to offer the water free gratis."

"Hmm, that is option one. Give me more time to contemplate that idea."

"I do not see any other option available than to demolish it for the property and rebuild the home of your dreams. With modern architecture and amenities."

"Damien, I could never consider that option. It has too much history and even if I did demolish it. People would still travel here looking for it. Then their hopes and dreams would be shattered. It needs to stay as it is."

"So, to be clear. You want to purchase the house but have no idea what to do with it afterwards. Correct?"

"Somewhat correct."

"You baffle me Maddison."

"Damien, I will find out how this water is healing people. If it truly does heal people or if it is a hoax and if that is the case, I will expose it and tell the world what we found."

"One problem, Annette has already proven to us."

"What is that?"

"The water fails to come out if you do not believe. Leading me to believe there

WATER

is a spiritual connection to the people drinking it."

"You are right, Damien. I failed to connect those dots."

"You are welcome."

"Go ahead lavish in your intelligence. I will give you credit for thinking outside the box. Albeit just this once."

"Ha! I knew you loved me. And if you ever stop. I'm spiking your drinks with the water."

"SERIOUSLY, DAMIEN"

WATER

Lancefield Stories

Annette's phone begins to ring. Picking up her new flip phone she answers.

"Hello this is Annette Lancefield."

"Miss Lancefield this is Maddison Graves. May we meet again for another viewing of your family's home today?"

"Yes Maddison, I am free today, what time are you thinking?"

"I am in front of the house now. Can you come now?"

'Yes I can. You will find a key under the yellow flowerpot on the right side of the front door on the porch. Let yourself in, I will be there shortly."

WATER

Maddison exits her car and walks up the short flight of stair that leads her past the mailbox onto the stone walkway to the front door. Holding her purse with one hand and her car keys in the other.

Stopping at the first step she looks at the mailbox and decides this mailbox thing is strange and makes the decision to ascend the three steps to the flat stone walkway. Meticulously she takes one step at a time until she is abreast of the mailbox. When an unknown force tugs on her purse almost dropping it. Composing herself she places the purse strap back into position at her bent elbow as she looks around for the mysterious cause of the unknown force that grabbed her purse.

No one was near her. No animals either. She was there all by herself. Shrugging off the encounter she picked up her pace and headed for the flowerpot at the front door.

Lifting the pot, she retrieved the key to insert it in the doors locked handle. Struggling to unlock the old door as the key found the ability to engage the tumblers. The door handle finally turns, opening the door giving way to her entrance.

WATER

Now inside the foyer, Maddison feels the same chilling air she experienced talking to Damien the night before. Despising him for choosing to play golf instead of accompanying her to see the house. Then quickly shrugging off her scorn for him, realizing she did give him the option and her blessing to do so.

She now regrets her decision and begins a slow walk into the room of photos. Passing thru the doorway that separates the foyer and the living room where the photos are tacked to the wall, she feels a pressure against her entire body that encompasses her almost causing her to faint in the process, then vanishing, releasing her when the front door opens.

Startled by the sound, Maddison quickly pirouettes to see Annette Lancefield entering the doorway.

"My dear, I did not mean to frighten you. Are you all right?"

"Yes. I did not expect you here so soon, I did not hear a vehicle pull up either. How did you get here?"

WATER

"A good friend was coming this way. So, I hitched a ride with him. You sure you are ok?"

"Yes I am fine, Although for a moment I had this eerie feeling of pressure on me. It is gone now. May I take a moment to look at these pictures once again and then I would like to go downstairs in the basement to have a look at that faucet you say produces magical water."

"Oh, Honey there is nothing magical about the water. The water heals the believers."

"Has it been tested for impurities or anything special in it?"

"You can't just go down there and draw a glass and take it somewhere to be tested."

"Why is that?'

"The faucet is aware if you are a believer or not. It will not produce a drop of water if you attempt to fill a glass for any other purpose than for healing."

"Annette, I am new to all of this, and I need time to comprehend the evidence you provide. Would you mind sharing more stories of the people displayed in these pictures?"

WATER

"Maddison, There have been many, many people come to this house requesting the water. They bring containers to be filled with the water, to take back with them wherever they've traveled from.

"It only works one on one in the basement with whoever is present. That is the only time it will provide the healing water."

"Do they leave disappointed?"

"The sad part is, Yes they do. Every new arrival is informed of how it works and and its potential to heal. But there are those that we cannot convince. We have never denied anyone an attempt to get the water out of the faucet. Many have tried to fill up the container they have brought with them. The faucet shuts down every time."

For a moment, the two women stood silent. Maddison began walking the room again peering into each photograph, hoping she could recognize someone from her childhood that may have used the water at some time in their life. It would give her some conviction lending merit to the stories the Lancefield's water actually produced the results Annette claims.

WATER

Annette stood silent, watching Maddison walked the room, viewing the photographs. Paying attention to the ones she briefly stopped in front of them in an attempt to gain more detail of a single photo.

Deliberating the importance of each person in the photograph, Maddison stops, picking one out a and pointing her finger at a specific photograph, she asks.

"This one, tell me about this little boy."

That is Benjamin, my father called him "Benny" he was brought to us by a nice couple who ran a foster home in the Virginia coal mine territory. He refused to have a good relationship with anyone and would not do as he was told. He was constantly in trouble for fighting at school.

The man and his wife tried everything they could think of to change his attitude. As with the others, they heard of the water from a friend.

They left him on the doorstep. My father did not think the water would help him with his attitude because he did not have a disease. Unable to take no! for an answer, they turned away and left him here with my father."

"That is a terrible thing to do to a child Annette, I find that hard to accept. The foster parents just left that little boy here. Without any remorse for doing so."

"Correct Maddison"

"What happened to him after they left?"

"We did not have an extra room for him so, my father found a neighbor to take him into their home. They had no children and made an agreement that Benjamin could stay with my father here during the day while they went off to work at the factory.

One day he went downstairs on his own discovering the faucet. Needing a drink of water, he turned on the faucet and drank the water from it."

"Let me guess Annette, his attitude changed after that."

"Indeed, it did. The neighbors were already skeptical of the water's ability to heal a person, no matter what problem they had. If they believed or were as innocent as Benjamin. It did its job."

"Annette, please tell me the rest of Benjamins story."

"Maddison, most of the time we never hear back from people who visit and drink the water, because Benjamin was under my father's watchful eye, we know the rest of his story."

"Go on tell me."

"Benny began doing his schoolwork and became a model classmate, graduating in the top of his class and securing a scholarship to the university of Virginia where he graduated with a law degree. If you buy the house, he will be the lawyer I will use for the closing."

Silently without responding, Maddison turned to take another look at the photo of 'Benny' now focusing on a signature of his name scribbled at the bottom of the photo in faded ink. Clearly Annette was telling another Lancefield family story.

WATER

The thought of what to make of all this danced in her head. Then she regained her walk to find another photo to challenge Annette's memory.

"This one here of the old lady. The photo looks older than the rest. What can you tell me of her?"

"Harriet. The meanest woman I personally have ever known."

"Mean? as in angry mean? Or worse than that?"

"Married three times, widowed three times, inherited a fortune three times. The fourth husband outsmarted her. He suspected she was poisoning him because of the terrible stomach problems he was having after eating her cooking. He came to my grandfather just before he felt he would pass away and asked to drink the water on a daily basis.

Harriet, caught on to him coming here for the water. I am guessing he wasn't following the protocol of the other three, so, she followed him here one day. I happened to answer the knock on the front door.

WATER

Maddison that was the first time I have ever experience a lady talk like she did to me, I got an earful from that woman."

Maddison could not control her laughter and asked.

"What did she say to you Annette?"

"I caught half of what she was saying until my grandfather walked up behind me and covered my ears, then proceeded to calm Harriet enough to invite her in for a drink of water herself.

He then led her to the staircase and gave her instructions of what to do when she found the faucet.

"I am sure there is a more to this Lancefield story. Please continue Annette."

"She must have been down there a little too long. My grandfather went to the basement door to cack it open to check on her. It seems the water kept flowing out of the faucet after she drank all she could and began filling the basement.

WATER

Evidently she was on her way up the stairs when Grandfather turned the handle to open the door. When he did, It burst open with Harriet coming out with a water-soaked dress up to her waist. She ran out of the house yelling that dam faucet was trying to drown me."

Chuckling with laughter, Madison had one final question.

"How much water was in the basement?"

"We do not know."

"What do you mean, it had to be waist deep if her dress was wet up to her knickers."

"The crazy part of this story is when my grandfather went back to the basement to access the water level. He witnessed the strangest event he had ever experienced with the faucet and the water that came from it."

"Well, what happened to the water?"

"Grandfather took a few steps into the basement and stopped."

WATER

"Why, Annette you have a weird look on your face. What happened to your grandfather?"

"What he witnessed was unbelievable to him as the water was receding."

"Where did it go?"

"Back into the faucet."

"No way."

"Maddison, I did not want to believe my grandfather's story. So, I went down there after he told me what he saw with his own eyes."

"How could that possibly happen."

"Maddison, I am telling you from my own account of what I saw when I stepped into the basement. All of the water was completely gone, and the floor was dry as the Sahara desert."

"I have to see this faucet now. Where is the basement doorway? Are you coming with me?"

"No, Maddison. You will have to go down there alone. I am not coming with you."

"Why not?"

"I refuse to go down there after that happened. I promise you; since that day I have refrained from entering the basement again."

"Ok then, I will go down there by myself."

Annette escorted Maddison to the basement door and stepped back several steps as Maddisson opened the door."

"Light switch is two steps down on your right. Good luck Maddisson."

"Now you're giving me concern, Annette."

Maddison Graves counted the two
steps and reached for the light switch and
lifted the small, toggled handle to energize

the electricity to the lone light hanging by a cord in the middle of the basement.

There it was on the left as Annette instructed, attached to the stone wall was a green oxidized faucet. Assuming it was made of brass, with an ornamental four spoke handle.

Maddison took the last step onto the concrete floor with extreme caution and advance towards the faucet and faced it head on.

The chilled air hit her once again, she was freezing in the basement environment that was normally a constant temperature all year long.

What had just happened to her? Thinking she never had these chills before being interested in this house. The temptation to turn on the valve was getting the best of her and with her right arm, she reaches out, placing her hand on the faucet's handle.

Maddison's hand immediately felt electrified, causing her arm to retract quickly when she senses movement off to her right side. Turning to investigate the possibility of the presence of something in the basement with her. Nothing presented itself. As Maddison returned towards the faucet.

Maddison made another attempt to turn on the faucets valve hoping the water would flow for her. Again, she felt the electrifying pulse radiating back thru her arm. This time she held tight to the spoked knob, opening it to release the water held back by the valve inside of it.

Nothing flowed from the faucet. Maddisson now considered she was being tricked by Annette and her mind pondered.

"This Is this nothing more than a game, a sinister hoax."

Thinking to herself. She considers her approach to the faucet may be portraying skepticism towards the process and could possibly be the cause for derailing its ability to produce the water.

Maddison assumed the worst-case scenario had been played out on her. Still standing at the faucet she began to fume. Then, she began talking to the faucet as if it could hear her.

"The stories Annette Lancefield told me, I believed in you mister magical faucet. I believed you could provide a power of healing with your water. If you want me to continue believing, give me some water even if it is a drop. I need to know if this is real or a hoax."

Moments pass; Maddison waits for her drop of water. Leaving the valve open, anticipating the arrival of the sign she asked for. The proof she needed to continue believing.

The time had come for Maddisson to leave the basement. Nothing came from the faucet. Not a single drop of liquid felled from the faucet into the old metal sink.

It was dead silence in the basement. Maddison could hear her own heartbeat cycle the blood flow in her body.

She turns to find the stairs. Prudently lifting her right foot up placing it on the first step.

She heard it.

The sound for which she had hoped. Turning back, she walked back to face the faucet. Tilted her head down, looking into the bottom of the sink.

WATER

There, to her amazement, was a tiny wet pool from a single drop of water. It was the confirmation she had requested.

Maddison smiled, she was now accepted as a believer.

Full of joy. Maddison graciously traversed the steps up and out the basement door to greet Annette still awaiting for her. Arms outstretched, she "embraced" Annette with her outstretched arms. Maddison was crying happy tears.

This was a new experience for Annette. No one had ever come from the basement after experiencing the faucet to "embrace" her in this manner.

"My dear Maddison. Are you ok? What happened to you down there?"

"I cannot explain it in words Annette. It was nothing like I have ever experience in my life."

"The water has that ability to change people forever. Now, Please let go of me Maddison."

"Oh! Yes, I am sorry I got carried away for a moment. Today's experience is enough for me; I need to leave now. I will contact you later this week to discuss the terms of the purchase. You can take the sign off the lawn."

"Ok, I can do that, and I shall await your call. Enjoy the rest of your day. I am sure you know your way out by now. Good day, Maddison,"

"Yes, Goodbye, Annette."

WATER

The Stake-out

{Sunday 8:00AM at the Country Club}

Damien pulls into the parking area of the country club. Leaving his clubs in the trunk of the car he walks into the clubhouse to meet the other three friends that will make up his Sunday foursome. After greeting his foursome and shaking hands Damien turns to Mitchel, his closest friend from college to ask a favor.

"Mitchel I need a favor."

"What happened Damien? Is Maddison holding back on your weekly allowance? I can cover you today if you need me too."

"No, it's not that. I do need to borrow your car though."

"Sure, you can. What are you planning to do with it?"

"Long story. I will fill you in later afterwards. I will be back before you finish at eighteen. Now let's swap keys."

Damien walks briskly out of the clubhouse to the parking lot and begins using Mitch's key fob to find where his vehicle was parked. Pressing the start button on the Nisson pathfinder and selecting drive he was off to initiate his stake-out plan.

The plan was simple. Borrow a friend's car and drive to the house Maddison is considering to purchasing. Once there, the plan is to sit in the car and observe any activity at the house. Hopefully undetected.

Turning onto the street he could see Maddison exiting the house, down portico steps and briskly walking the stone pathway towards the mailbox. Then for some reason she stops short and alters her intended path away from the mailbox.

WATER

Finding a suitable parking spot. He shut off the car and slouched low in the seat where he could barely see over the steering wheel so Maddison could not bust him.

Getting caught by her would end his relationship with her for good. Damien figured as a man he needed to do what he deemed necessary to protect her from getting scammed out of her inheritance.

This house and the stories about people getting healed from drinking water from a faucet in a basement seemed like the perfect set-up for her to get drained of her money. Damien knew her father's brother well enough that it would be just like him to set up this type of scam. If he somehow found out she was interested in purchasing it.

Damien sits quietly in stealth mode watching his fiancé drive away, when Annette stepped out onto on the porch, watching as Annette turns to lock the door and then places the key under a yellow planter. Turning away from the door she begins her exit from the house by carefully stepping down the steps to the stone pathway leading to the mailbox.

"Here is the first test. He says to himself. If she walks past that mailbox, I will have the first piece of evidence I need."

Annette closes in on the mailbox then suddenly changed her course as she did before. Veering away from the intended path. Using the sloped grass lawn to reach someone in a parked vehicle waiting for her. Opening the passenger door and slipping in.

Damien watches the rear brake lights flicker on then off as the car's driver pulls away from the house.

Undeterred from his stake-out. Remaining in position, watching and waiting for some evidence. Just then he notices an older couple walking towards the house after crossing the street. Seemingly in a hurry they place flowers at the base of the steps then hurried back across the street to continue their walk like nothing had happened.

Damien thought this was a bit strange as he penciled the episode on a notepad. No sooner had the first couple leave. Another couple following the same path. Except this couple ran across the street to leave an envelope in the mailbox, then followed the same stealth style protocol back across the street to continue to an unknown destination.

Making quick notes with his pencil, Damien lifts his head to look back at the house.

"Not again he says to himself."

Next a middle-aged man drives up to the house. Parking his car while leaving the engine running and quickly exits the vehicle to jog up to the steps to leave what appears to be a bank zippered money bag on the porch next to the yellow planter and returning hastily back to his vehicle to drive away.

Damien makes note after note of the activity for the next two hours. Some visitors put envelopes in the mailbox while others left a memento or flowers on the porch.

Three hours have passed since he arrived to begin the stake-out. It was now time for him to leave the area and return to the golf course and return his friend's car. Placing his foot on the brake he looks down to find the start button directing his finger to push the button when a man appears from the back of the house to begin collecting the gifts and placing the flowers in a bag then heads to the mailbox to retrieve the contents left behind by several of the temporary visitors.

Damien resists the urge to step out of the car and confront the man. knowing if he did, it would create a bigger problem he was not ready to address at the moment.

Damien looks back down to locate the push to start button as he continues his fingers travelling towards the red button and drives himself back the the country club to meet his friend Mitchel.

Arriving at the moment his friends are finishing at the eighteenth green, Damien waves at the group and motions to meet him at the nineteenth watering hole inside the clubhouse.

Mitch settles in next to Damien at the table and signs his scorecard, then looks up at Damien as the waiter brings a round of drinks for the two of them.

"Ok 5-0 what the hell were you doing with my car. I am sure you were either sneaking around on Maddison, which I do hope is not the case here or you are spying on her, thinking she is cheating on you. Which is it?"

Taking a sip of his crown royal and coke. Damien wisely selects his response.

"It is neither of the above."

Mitch is gravely concerned for Damien; this is not his modus operandi as he leans in to click glasses with his friend and asks.

"Then what is this about? You two are scheduled to be married soon. Are you getting cold feet? Better question here, is Maddison getting cold feet and you are running scared? You've asked me to be your best man. So, spill the beans."

"Mitch, I do not know if you will believe me or understand what I am about to tell you, and please keep this between you and I. Promise? I am banking on our attorney client relationship."

"Oh well in that case if you are retaining me as your lawyer then I will plead insanity if this goes south on you."

WATER

Mitch agreed to Damien's request. The two men talked for hours as Damien poured his heart out to Mitch about the house and the recent findings. To which Damien asks.

"Tell me what you think Mitch."

"I think I need another cocktail."

"On your membership account and I will have another with you."

Mitch holds his thoughts in silence as other members walk past their table. Once clear Mitch reveals his take on the house deal and Maddison's behavior after her father's funeral.

"First question Damien. Did she request a pre-nuptial agreement?"

"Jokingly yes, in reality, no she is not requiring it."

"You have dodged a bullet with that one."

"You forget Mitch she passed the bar."

'Oh, yes, we actually took the test the same day. So, here is some advice. It does not matter. That is daddy's money and now it is her money. Wether she includes you in her purchases or not, remember one thing."

"What is that?"

"It is her money first and you are an afterthought. So, ride the white horse and shut up."

Stunned at Mitch's take on the conversation. Damien chugs the last bit of his cocktail then responds accordingly."

"Thanks for the reality check Mitch, I will be heading home now."

Damien rises from the table, pushes his chair back, turns and takes a couple steps away when he hears Mitch ask."

"Will you be continuing the stake-out activity?"

WATER

Stopping in his track and without turning to address his friend Damien replies.

"You bet I am."

'I Figured you would. Be careful and do not get caught."

"Not planning on it."

Mitch lets Damien walk away then mumbles under his breath.

"No one ever does."

{Monday, 10:00AM Maddison wakes up to the smell of coffee.}

Dressing herself before taking the stairs down to the kitchen. She knows her man all too well. He is the perfect gentleman. Letting himself in with the key she gave him years ago. He knows the routine. Make some coffee and start brunch. She will not come down until she is ready, and he is not to come up under any circumstance to wake her.

Stepping off the staircase. Maddison walks over to her favorite placement at the kitchen Island. It is the best seat in the house. It is where she has the best view of her man preparing her coffee with something to eat. She starts the conversation.

"What did you bring today? I am hungry and missed your cooking last night. Golf must have been tiring for you. You did not text either."

Damien was feeling nervous in front of Maddison. After a night's sleep he considered he may have made a mistake with the surveillance. Turning toward Maddison trying not to show his emotions. He decided to create a subject line of questions, hoping to throwing her off his scent.

"How was your visit with Annette yesterday?"

"Fine, I went into the basement to check out the faucet all by myself."

WATER

"I am proud of you. How was the experience?"

"Not so bad, How was it driving Mitch's car?"

"Not so bad."

Damien replies in a soft tone. Hoping she did not see him down the street and maybe she spotted him driving back to the golf course. More silence filled the otherwise talkative mornings together.

Maddison breaks first to ask.

"Did you see anything suspicious at the house?"

Damien is, BUSTED.

Damien grabs his cup of coffee to sit at the island across from Maddison. She lifts her head and twists it to the side to reposition her coal black hair away from her eyes in order to have a clear view of Damien. The stern look from her squinting eyes, and the pursed lips were too much for Damien to ignore. It was now time to confess what he was up too.

"It is all about you and me. If I am going to be your husband it is my duty to protect you. In any manner, I see fit. I can see this has upset you, but you will have to get over it and accept it. End of discussion."

Maddison sits up and leans back in the high-top chair to take in Damiens response with direct eye contact and replies.

"You have grown a set. A big set. Thank you for being my knight in armor. I actually do appreciate and love you for taking the initiative."

Damien was taken back at Maddison's admission. He never thought she would react in a positive manor towards him for sneaking around behind her.

"I love you Maddison and I do want the best for you and our future together as husband and wife. I had to do what I had to do."

"Great now put your coffee down Damien and follow me upstairs to the bedroom, you need rewarding my protector."

{3:00PM. Monday, A call to Mitch}

"Hello Damien, I figured you would be calling soon."

"How would you know, I would call?"

"You got busted didn't you?"

"Yes, again, I ask. How do you know this?"

"Maddison called my wife to ask why you were driving my car yesterday instead of playing golf. She obviously went on a fishing expedition after she saw my car and you in it at the end of the street. You didn't figure in your scheme, those two go shopping together using my car."

"I got it now, The reason for my call was to figure out how she knew."

"How did she react?"

"Let me put it this way Mitch."

"Blah, Blah, Blah. No details please "D." I can conclude by the sound of your voice you must have been rewarded in lieu of getting booted out of the house during your morning coffee routine."

"You know about our routine?"

"Good by Damien, see you next Sunday at the club."

{5:00 PM Monday. More surveillance}

Damien arrives at the house in his own black Toyota SUV. Parking in the same spot he decided to watch for any activity that may happen in the afternoon.

It was no surprise to witness the exact same activity repeating itself in the afternoon. Except this time, something was quite different when Father Levi makes an appearance in front of the house. Bringing a few followers with him.

Bowing their heads together on the sidewalk in front of the mailbox to begin a prayer. Afterwards Father Levi steps up to the mailbox and retrieves a small number of envelopes previously placed inside.

Turning back to his followers he distributes an envelope to each one of them as they then depart in separate directions.

Damien continues to watch the activity at the house when he sees the same person from before coming from the back of the house and retrieves the flowers and gifts left by well-wishers and those who have previously experienced the "water."

Unable to conclude who this person is. Damien is amazed to see the person walk the stone pathway down to the mailbox to ensure the contents had been removed, then disappeared to the back of the house with his collection of gifts.

This was enough for today's surveillance. Damien starts his vehicle and heads home to Maddison.

WATER

{7:18PM Damien drives home.}

I Have Questions

{9:00AM   Wednesday   morning coffee}

Damien pours two cups of coffee, one for him and one for Maddison. Setting her cup in front of her, she immediately picks it up blowing softly on the dark liquid, then takes in the aroma with her nose before the first sip.

Damien repeats the same procedure. The air is thick. Maddison senses something is amiss. She waits for her morning companion to begin conversing on his terms.

Both repeat the performance of drinking hot coffee together when

Maddison decides the Mexican standoff must come to an end.

She asks.

"What is troubling you, my love?"

"When are you meeting Annette again to discuss the purchase price?"

"Later today I believe she said 5:00PM."

"I can drive you if you wish."

"I thought you had lost interest in the house. You have been working Five-O trying to derail it. I understand you want to be my savior, but I want the house whether we live in it or not. Does that somehow make sense to you?"

"Yes it does. Although you are wrong, I am not trying to "derail it" as you described. A little trust in me would be appreciated. There has been a flurry of activity at that house daily. More than I have divulged to you."

"Spill the beans as they say, Mr. investigator."

"Glad you have a sense of humor Maddison. Especially towards what I have been doing. I did not expect you to approve."

"If, I did not love and trust you, I would have buried you in the back yard already. Now continue with the evidence. I like playing judge and jury."

Damien and Maddison share a laugh, then he fills her ears with mounds of information. Damien brings out his notepad. The insurance executive now turned into a private investigator begins presenting the evidence written down in his notepad. Maddison is impressed with his due diligence.

"Wow, You have more information than I thought. I am impressed with your discovery. You missed your calling by not enrolling in the police academy."

"I do not think so Maddison. I would not be the right person sent out to council domestic disputes. I will ask you this. Do you want to ask Annette, about all this activity, or should I?"

"I am going to let you be the bad cop this time."

"Gee thanks Maddison. I am feeling loved."

"Not this morning Damien, I have a headache."

"You have never said that to me, before now."

"I am practicing for when we get married."

"I see."

{5:00PM The house.}

Arriving at the house, Maddison looks out of the passenger window to see Annette standing on the porch with a well-dressed younger man in a suit and tie.

Exiting his side of the car, Damien takes a good look at the two waiting for them on the porch before opening the passenger door for Maddison. Reaching for the handle, Damien opens the heavy door of the El Camino. Maddison steps out to stand next to her chauffeur.

The two are now standing outside of the car. Maddison takes Damiens' hand to pull him in close to whisper a few words before they venture up to the house.

"I would like to see you in a suit like that man on the porch more often. Those golf shirts you wear are old and stained."

Damien is stunned by her admission, then takes in her advice and jokingly replies to Maddison.

"Yes Miss Daisy. I sure will do as you say."

Maddison shakes off his response with a giggle as they proceed to the portico share. Approaching the steps of the porch. Annette announces a greeting.

"Welcome back you two. I have a special guest to introduce to the two of you.

Benjamin, say hello to Maddison Graves and Damien Steele. These are my potential buyers."

Damien and Maddison immediately stop walking at the foot of the stairs and stand shocked on the final piece of stone walkway before stepping up the three steps to where Annette and Benjamin await.

Neither could believe what they are encountering. Maddison had her confirmation of Annete Lancefield's stories. Realizing the man next to her was also displayed in one of the photos on the wall she inquired about.

Damien recognizes this is the man who has been removing the gifts left by well-wishers. Even with the distance he viewed the house. He has confirmation who the person was.

Annette commands.

"Come up, the both of you. Let us go inside so we may negotiate a fair asking price for this lovely home. Come now, inside with you."

WATER

Strangely enough both Damien and Maddison's feet felt as if they were solidly glued to the one stone under their feet. They were unable to move until Annette and Benjamin turned away from them.

Instantly they were released to follow their host into the house. Damien, being a gentleman allowed Maddison to enter the door ahead of him. Trailing her from behind, Damien moves in close enough to hold her back slightly with one hand placed around her waist to lean in and whisper in her right ear.

"What just happened to us?"

Maddison leans her head back towards him replying in a whisper.

"I don't know."

Entering the foyer and moving swiftly into the living room of photos. Benjamin stands proud by himself in the middle of the room. Maddison walks up to him to take a close look at his face and then at the younger photo of him on the wall, confirming it is indeed the Benjamin in the photo pinned to the wall.

She then proceeds to walk around him in a 360-degree circle examining every inch of him.

She closes within his personal space. Benjamin feels Maddison's breath on his neck. Breaking the rooms' tranquility.

He asks.

"Miss Graves, would you like to touch me, to see if I am a real person?"

Maddison takes a few steps back away from Benjamin. Looking over at Damien with a stark expression of surprise he does not recognize.

Annette moves close to Maddison and seizes the opportunity to express her gratitude to for coming to the house today to negotiate the asking price. Annette reaches out with her right hand to gently contact Maddison's left arm. She guides her away from Benjamins' personal space.

Annette replies:

"Maddison, I must admit, I am not particularly good at real estate negotiating. So, If you do not mind, I have asked Benjamin to negotiate in good faith for me.

He is a good closing attorney and very proficient in real estate transactions. Is that acceptable to you?"

Maddison has not removed her gaze from Benjamin the entire time they have been standing in the room of photographs. She begins her reply to Annette without looking away from her subject.

"Yes of course Miss Lancefield."

"Oh, thank you. The two of you can sit at the kitchen table to discuss the provisions of the sale. Benjamin has his briefcase with all the paperwork on the table already. Off with the two of you, go on now."

Annette places each of her hands on the lower back of both Maddison and Benjamin to start their journey into the Kitchen.

As commanded the two leave the room for the kitchen. Benjamin leads the way with Maddison following close behind. She stops briefly to glance back at Damien with a bewildered expression.

Damien is alone with Annette when she starts a conversation with him.

"Is there anything we can discuss while they are in the Kitchen?"

"Yes there is. I HAVE QUESTIONS!"

"If it pleases you Damien, we can go out on the portico to chat."

Damien walks over to point at one of the photographs.

"That is fine with me, but before we leave this room of photographs. I am intrigued with the stories you've told us about the people in these photos. I would like for you to tell me the story about this man here dressed in the old-style military uniform."

"Yes, of course. That is Sargent Reynolds. He came to see my grandfather some eight years after his discharge from the Army at the end of World War II. He was one of the men landing at Normandy Beach."

"Annette. I am sure he had a reason for coming here, I assume he drank from the faucet like the others, "seeking a cure." Did he also have a specific problem like everyone else before him?"

"Mr. Steele, I sense you have trouble believing in the power of the water. Are you with faith Damien Steele?"

"I question the process you have in place and "Yes" Annette, you have no need to question my faith. Although I have little confidence in the validity of your stories "Miss Lancefield. And, I have a few more questions to ask you."

"Let me finish telling you about Sargent Reynolds first and then, I will field your remaining questions."

"Yes, of course. Carry on."

"You see, Mr. Reynolds struggled mentally with the war. Unable to clear his head of the carnage that day. Many of the men in his platoon were lost during the first hours of the battle. He somehow survived without a scratch.

WATER

That alone troubled him with the burning question of "why" was he spared? Why did he survive when so many others did not? He was on the verge of taking his own life when someone referred him here for "healing" thru the power of the "water." He then had a reason to seek out the water.

He arrived a broken man with deeply rooted depression. My grandfather listened to his story before leading him to the basement door and as with everyone else. Gave him the same instructions."

"You are to stand in front of the faucet. Turn it on. If the water flows. Drink it. Then, come back up here. I will let you return as many times as you need. When you feel you are healed. You are not to return.

For two weeks he came to meet with my grandfather. After that, we never saw him again until his photograph was delivered with the mail. The accompanying note told the story of how he is now a healed man."

Damien still skeptically responds kindly to Annette.

WATER

"Inspiring story Miss Lancefield. May we now go out on the portico and discuss the other questions I have."

"Yes of course. Follow me Mr. Steele."

Annette leads the way out onto the porch where two rocking chairs await. Annette directs Damien with a wave of her hand to use one of the chairs while she sits at the other.

"Please sit Damien. You may now ask your remaining questions."

"First; I must be honest with you. I have taken it upon myself to engage in a stake-out this house. Watching all of the activity from afar down the street, just to observe what is happening."

"I see. Let me guess the questions you would like to begin with?. Where do the flowers go? Or what about the gifts left behind? Oh yes; I am sure you are genuinely concerned about the money left in the mailbox or under the planter?"

"Yes, Those are the questions I have. How do you know what I was about to ask you?"

WATER

"Young man you are not the first person who has been here to inquire, nor will you be the first person to come back to surveil the house. My father and his father have both been questioned by nay-sayers and by local authorities many times over.

A plethora of people before you have investigated this place for a hundred years or more. Especially when we elect a new sherif in town. They always seem hell bent on proving something is amiss out here."

"I get that Annette. I am not the first person that has questioned the legitimacy of the water?"

"Nor will you be the last Damien. Nor will you be the last."

"I understand your point to my questioning. Please explain what do you do with the flowers and the gifts? Maddison will need to know this when she takes possession."

"Let me put your mind at ease. You see, Benjamin lives behind this house on the opposite side of the hedgerow. Every day he comes thru the back hedgerow and collects the articles left behind. He takes care of this for me.

WATER

There are an enormous number of people and places needing a fresh bouquet of flowers. To cheer people up, Benny takes them to the local nursing home. He sometimes "prints" the names of relatives on a card when he can find out who their relatives are.

This gives them comfort that their relatives care about their situation, even though the relatives never visit in person. He also distributes them to grave sites and funeral homes. Especially for the john doe funerals.

The gifts he takes are a different story all together. He takes them to the homeless and to the children waiting for adoption at the orphanage, as for the money, it is a donation. It goes to Father Levi to be distributed to the needy who have no job and to those needing help to pay bills or to buy food.

Am I providing the necessary answers to satisfy your questions?"

"I must stress this again Annette. Maddison needs to know all of this before she purchases this house."

"Calm yourself my son, Benjamin is explaining all of this now to her as we speak. We will know her decision shortly."

126

WATER

"Annette, I now have a better understanding of the need for this house and what it has become to the community and to certain people. No one should change that for which it is used. Quietly it serves the needy and people who believe in the "water.""

"Yes Damien, especially the power of the "water." The spirit controls that.""

"Spirit? Annette, you have emphasized they must believe in its power to heal. Or it will not help them.""

"That is correct Damien.""

"So, to add to the mystique about the "water" you've elected to display photographs of the people who make testament to its ability it has healed them in some way. Am I correct to assume, you need this display in order to convince the new arrivals the "water" is legitimate?""

"Once again Damien, I must admit you are assuming we do this oddly like a commercial investment. I will assure you it is not. I cannot express enough to you what I am about to say to you. You can "never" break the cycle of believing in the "water.""

WATER

If you do, you will destroy the belief of thousands of followers that have already consumed the water and fully believe the "water" healed them.

Furthermore, you will destroy the hope, dreams and faith of thousands of people who have yet to arrive at this house for their belief the "water" has the ability to heal the sickness with which they are stricken.

No other person can know the truth. You cannot tell anyone, not even your fiancée Maddison. Once again, I say to you. You cannot break the cycle. Can you promise me this Damien Steele?"

"Yes: I believe I can, although, I have one last question, Annette."

"I know what that question will be. No need to ask it, although, I can see it is an itch that is getting the best you. Go ahead, Damien Steele, ask it."

"You just mentioned, no one should know the truth, So, how do you turn the water on from upstairs while they are downstairs?"

"It is all about your "faith" Mr. Steele. I promise you too will be a believer. Now, Benjamin should be finishing with your fiancée any moment. Do you have my phone number, Damien? Before we end our meeting, you are welcome to call me anytime you have a question regarding the house. I assume you will be the "man" of the house. I do have your word on this. Do I not?"

"Yes Miss Lancefield. You have my word."

"Good, now let us go back inside and see if the two of them have reached an agreement."

"If you do not mind Annette: I need to sit out here for a moment to collect my thoughts. You can go in and find out that answer yourself, I will follow shortly."

"Yes, of course. What I have said and asked of you, is a lot to digest. To make myself clear. You and I have spoken confidentially. I will deny everything spoken by me if you decide to change your mind. See you inside Damien."

WATER

With those parting words Annette steps inside to greet Maddison and Benjamin in the kitchen.

Damien sits in the rocking chair for an additional amount of time. Readying himself to stand. He cannot move from the chair. He is locked in. A swift chilling breeze begins to blow across his body.

Quickly it is suppressed and he can now stand up with his own power. Thinking nothing of the wind. Damien Steele enters the house to join the others.

WATER

The two spirits

{2:00AM two days later.}

Damien encounters insomnia as he lay awake in bed next to Maddison. He has remaining questions about the house he cannot get off of his mind. These questions are causing him sleepless nights. His Maddison is content with the purchase, but his concerns and questions remain unanswered.

{9:00AM a call to Annette.}

Damien finishes his morning coffee with Maddison when he informs her he is heading out for work. Kissing his wife to be he heads to his car. With his lack of sleep, he yawns before the car starts. Reaching for the stick shifter to place it in reverse. The back-up camera lights up the display screen. Damien immediately applies the brakes when he realizes he had forgotten to open the garage door.

Settling his nerves now that the garage door is safely up and out of the way, he backs out of the garage and drives away from his house.

Arriving at his insurance company he settles in at his desk and picks up the phone to dial Annette Lancefield.

"Miss Lancefield. I have a few more questions regarding the house. May we meet for lunch today, away from the house if you agree?"

"Yes, I am available today. Let's meet for pizza. I have not had a good pie in a long time. I do believe you know of a good place?"

WATER

"As a matter of fact, I do. I will see you at twelve O'clock."

Damien purposefully refrains from mentioning his and Maddison's favorite place to have pizza together, just to see if Miss Lancefield knows more than she lets on too.

Damien parks in front of Denino's and steps out of his car. Turning back towards the driver's door he uses the key to lock the door. A female voice breaks his concentration, startling him as he realizes the woman was directly behind him. Swiftly he turns around to see Annette standing less than a foot away.

Causing him to abruptly lean backwards on to the driver's door in order to gain some personal space.

"Miss Lancefield, You startled me. Where did you come from? I did not see you when I stepped out of the car just now."

Annette stares at Damien Her gray hair is flowing in the wind as she quickly prevents her dress from presenting an unpleasant situation. A few seconds pass when she takes control of the situation.

"Get a grip on yourself young man. The wind is terrible out here. Come, let's go inside. I am starving."

"Yes of course Miss Lancefield."

Damien composes himself while standing erect and begins to lead the way to the front door. Inside Damien informs the wait staff it will be the two of them. Requesting a table in the back away from the noise and crowd. They are led to a small table isolated from everyone else.

"Thank you Miss Lancefield for meeting with me on short notice. But I have a few more questions I need answered before we move on."

"Can we order first and when the pie arrives you can begin interrogating me with your questioning."

"Fair enough. Please tell the wait staff what you prefer on your pizza."

WATER

Turning his attention to the waitress, Damien instructed the young lady it would be one check today. Annette could not resist making a comment as she agrees Damien is the man paying the tab today. Cutting her eyes at Damien when she walks away with the order. Damien smirks and settles in for the questioning.

"Miss Lancefield, I…"

Annette quickly cuts Damien off before he can finish his first question. She has been thru this before and fears this meeting is to inform her the sale is a no go when she blurts out.

"Your fiancée has signed a contract with me to purchase the house. If you back out at this point, you will not get your earnest money returned to you. Pease refer to page six, Paragraph three."

"Miss Lancefield, Annette, we are not reneging on the contract. That is not the purpose of our luncheon."

WATER

"Well, if you are not trying to cancel the contract and ask for your deposit returned, then, what are we here for?"

Damien pauses himself before he begins his questioning. His pause is to give himself time to speak to Annette so as not to offend her with his tone when he does begin. Now ready he opens up the dialogue with how he feels when he is in the photo room.

"Annette, I have a confession to make. So, please help me understand the vibes I get when I enter the living room lined with photos."

Annette changes her attitude now that Damien has convinced her the sale of the house she hoped for was finally happening.

"Please Damien, tell me how you feel when you are with the spirit?"

"SPIRIT, you said SPIRIT."

137

WATER

"Yes, if you had not figured it out already you might as well be of knowledge there is a spirit that comes with the purchase of the home. I figured you knew one exists because of the interaction of the "water" from the faucet."

Damen is speechless. He knew Annette was holding back on something. He had yet to figure out the real game her family had been playing on people for years.

He stepped up the intensity of his questioning when he confessed he did not believe the pictures were real.

"Tell me Annette. Using your own words, I quote, "It is just the two of us here talking together." Tell me more about how I am supposed to use the ruse of this spirit to convince people they are healed from drinking the "water."

"Mr. STEELE! Let me tell you a thing or two about that house and the resident "spirit" you will have firsthand knowledge of soon enough. When it reveals itself to you, there will no longer be a doubt in your mind it is no "ruse" as you refer."

"My apology Miss Lancefield. I do not mean to offend you in any way. It is just this, I am not yet convinced any spirit exists in the home. Further I believe your family has played a sinister game for three generations."

"Mr. Damien Steele, I promise you. When you move in, the spirit of the house that controls the "water" will reveal itself to you. It has come forward to my grandfather and my father as it has revealed itself to me.

Be aware it is not the only spirit on the property. So, you are aware beforehand the spirit inside is the fair one to deal with."

"Are you now telling me I have more than one to deal with?"

"I indirectly mentioned the one at the mailbox to Maddison. It is the evil one. Stay clear of the mailbox if you or Maddison want to live a long time."

WATER

Damien sits stunned at Annette's confession of the spirits he needs to contend with when he responds.

"I see. Two spirits and one warning to stray away from the mailbox. Am I correct in my assumption?"

'Thank you for the Pizza Mr. Steele. I need to leave you now. Everything I have conveyed to you is real and true. If you do not believe me then I pray you survive longer than anyone. But I submit it to you. You will not. Good luck to you and Maddison."

With her last statement Annette left the table. Leaving Damien to ponder his next move. He is a man of his word and will not expose what he has learned to Maddison. He concludes that he may never find the right time to have a serious discussion with Maddison about his concerns for her purchase of the Lancefield home.

WATER

The Purchase

{Maddison's house 9:30AM the next day}

Damien walks in the front door of Maddison's house after stopping at the grocery store for a new bag of coffee. Walking into the house he notices, Maddison is already dressed and sitting at the island bar in the kitchen awaiting his arrival.

"You are up early my love."

"Yes, I could not sleep last night."

"Are you already having second thoughts about buying the house?"

"No!"

142

"That is a short answer from a woman who always has a lengthy opinion."

"Please get the coffee started, I need it this morning."

Without replying. Damien turns away from Maddison. He has learned after years together with her it is best to leave her be when she is rendering her morning emotion. He knows her well. A couple cups of coffee, and she will snap out of her mood soon enough. He comforts her with his words.

"Five minutes Maddison, Coffee in five."

Maddison is quiet. Pondering many thoughts in her head. The house is purchased. The question remains, what to do with it? The heavy lifting begins with the right decision and she knows it.

Raising her head up from her slumber to find the backside of Damien sticking out of the fridge and the other half of him inside looking for food to cook her for breakfast. She pauses her thinking to view his backside. Not hungry, she expresses her thoughts.

"If you are looking for food to cook. Do not bother. I am not hungry this morning. But thank you for initiating."

Damien stands erect to slowly close the door. The cold refrigerated air briefly felt good to him. Now he must deal with Maddison's morning.

When Maddison asks:

"Damien, do you love me?"

Damien turns his head towards her. She has never asked such a question. He quickly deliberates his answer:

It must be powerful enough at this moment to make a difference or he is toast.

Walking the two full strides to the island he stands in front of his princess. Her black hair frames the emotion displayed like a tv screen on her face. She is close to tears when he replies.

"Maddison. I have never loved anyone as much as, I do you and "I doubt"

144

I will ever love another as much, if you were to leave me."

"Perfect answer my love. Although, I need to know, Did I make the right decision?"

Damien realized at that moment it is time for him to be her rock. She no longer has her father, and her mother has never been there to nurture or mentor motherly instinct to her as she grew into a mature woman.

He has to assume the role of being the one person she can go to in her time of need: This is one of those times. Choosing his response wisely will make or break her, he cannot bear to see his Maddison broken.

"Maddison my darling. You bought a special house; it was a difficult decision to make alone with no mentorship at your side. Annette Lancefield is frail and understands it will take a special someone to carry on what her father and grandfather have built.

WATER

Those men believed in what the "water" could do for people. You have heard the stories; you experienced the power of the faucet firsthand yourself with the single drop of it in the sink."

"That was the proof you needed, it changed and convinced you: it solidified your belief. The "water" has changed thousands of people before you. It created a following of believers from people who needed answers. It gave them hope when they lost faith in doctors. It supported the belief they could be healed just by drinking the "water."

That house has given common people a place to come to when they needed help during the worst of times in their life. It gave them hope everything would be all right if they just drank from the faucet. Maddison, it is now you who must carry on the legacy of the "water."

"Thank-you for supporting me and my decision. I want to live in the house, can you see yourself living there with me?"

"Maddison Graves, I would live with you in a tent in the woods if it made you happy."

146

WATER

"Let's not go that far Damien."

"You get my meaning."

"Yes I do, now can we have coffee?"

"Coming right up."

"I adore how much you love and take care of me."

"If I didn't I would bury you in the back yard."

"Touché' Damien."

"Sorry; I had to go there."

"One more question "D.""

"Ask me anything."

"What are we going to name your son?"

Damien drops his coffee cup on the floor after hearing Maddison's question.

"Sorry Damien, I did not mean to shell shock you, I will help you clean that up. Let me get the paper towels for you."

Damien holds up his hand as a stop sign.

WATER

"Stay right there Maddison, I see you are barefoot and there are broken pieces of my cup on the floor. I got this."

Madison sits back in her chair watching her hero clean up the broken pieces and mop the floor. Damien holds back from asking Maddison to "clarify" her statement until he is finished. Retrieving a new cup from the cabinet then pours himself a fresh cup of coffee: asking Maddison if she requires a refill.

"Yes, of course I want more. I also want more of you when we finish our coffee."

"I'm all in on that."

"Ok, Damien. You have not asked for clarification on my shocking statement that caused you to drop your coffee cup. Are you afraid to ask or what?"

"Do I need clarification? Are you indeed pregnant with my child? Because if you are I am now the happiest man alive."

"No silly man, I am not pregnant. But If I were to have your child I would prefer a boy for you to raise to be the image of yourself."

"Please elucidate your reasoning for that decision, and for the shocking statement that is now false, Maddison."

"We women need more men like you. So hopefully one day we can have one or two "boys" to share with future women of the world."

"You never cease to amaze me Maddison."

Maddison giggles.

"I know."

"May I ask, when are you planning to close on the house?"

"A month from now. I gave her plenty of time to get her stuff out that she wanted or possibly change her mind. She liked that I gave her that option and the amount of Ernest money I believe sealed the deal."

"I doubt she will change her mind. What are you thinking of doing to the house for us to live in it? It is quite old and needs a lot of upgrades. I am not much of a handyperson if you are thinking I am your guy for that."

"I agree with you. We will have to secure a contractor. But the outside needs to stay within the historical period of architecture. Inside I can manage updating."

"What do you plan to do with the Photographs?"

"My love today is not the day for a lot of questions. If you are you finished with coffee."

"Say no more. Meet you upstairs in five."

{11:00 AM. At the house}

Damien pulls up to the house. Curiously, he walks up the stone walkway after a brief stop at the mailbox to ponder what special power that thing must "possess" adds a chuckle to his thoughts about the spirit that may have residence inside of it. Proceeding to the front steps and on to the porch to look for the key where Maddison said it should be.

Retrieving it he heads for the locked door but stops short to turn around. There at the foot of the steps behind him lay a bouquet of flowers.

How did those get there he wondered to himself. Then assumed he must have walked right past them not noticing their existence. Except he would have stepped on them where they were laying.

Stepping back down the steps he gathered them up and set them on one of the rocking chairs. Approaching the front door of the house once again to unlock the handle.

The lock would not budge as he began to phrase adjectives out loud to describe his frustration when the tumblers succumbed to the key.

Now inside the house, Damien begins his mission to find out how the water faucet works. Beginning his search at the doorway leading into the basement. Figuring the person upstairs has to know when the subject is in front of the faucet, But how?

The door is solid; It is void of peepholes anywhere, no apparent cracks in the door either. Thinking maybe the keyhole gives the person the ability to look in. Stooping down he peers thru the small skeleton keyway that locks the handle. It will not allow him to see down, only straight ahead. How are they doing this?, he asks himself.

Damien searches with his finger for an electrical button to turn on the faucet, running his fingers along the molding of the door. Feeling the old dry cracked caulking for a switch that may be hidden or embedded in it.

Nothing is found at the frame. Looking at the floor, he uses his feet to find a possible pressure point placed within the flooring that may activate a valve somehow. To his avail, nothing will make the "water" flow from the faucet.

Now walking around the kitchen for any evidence that may lend a clue to the mystery he cannot solve. Annette knows something she is not telling him.

Now leaving the kitchen he looks back one more time at the door leading to the basement where the magical faucet is attached to the exterior wall.

His mind ponders for a moment. It has to be something that is activating it from the basement. Damien finds the light switch, descends to the basement, and begins a search of the cold damp room.

Unable to find the smoking gun, he faces the faucet with dismay. The protocol is the same when he begins to address the "faucet" on a personal level.

"Something is not kosher here. I have faith and I am a believer. But you Mr. Faucet are a mystery to me. I promise you; I have to find how you work soon enough."

Nothing flows from the faucet. Damien leaves the basement and turns out the light.

Walking into the living room filled with photos of the believers. He sees men, women and children. All of their eyes seem to stare out at him, begging to share their individual story of how the power of the "water" interacted with their lives.

Skeptical, he walks around the room until he stops in front of a photograph of two men standing together as if they were one. The photo is old and torn on one side. A closer look reveals someone had been removed from the photo by tearing away a part of it.

"Why" he asks openly with his own voice.

Damien believing he is alone in the house, is startled when he hears a voice behind him respond to his question "Why."

"They removed their abusive father from the photo" the voice announces.

Scared out of his thoughts, Damien spins around to see who had followed behind him into the room. No one was there.

"I know, I heard a voice he tells himself." Assuming someone is now playing a game with him. Damien briskly walks in and out of each room frantically searching for the source of the vocals he heard behind him.

No one is in the house.

It was time to leave this place: Maddison is waiting on his report.

Reaching for the handle to open the front door he sees Benjamin thru the door's small pane of glass. He is removing flowers that were placed on the chair and the steps while he was in the house. Now assuming it was his voice he heard. He questions how Benjamin, was he able to disappear so quietly from the room and "quickly" enough he did not see him when he pivoted around?

Damien quickly opens the door to bolt out and confront Benjamin who is shocked to see Damien standing tall above him on the porch.

Damien yells out!

"Were you in the house just now? Why did you answer me like that, how did you get out here without me hearing your footsteps on the wooden floors? Tell me now!"

"Mr. Steele I have not been in the house today. You are mistaken; I came to retrieve the flowers. That is all I am here for. Miss Lancefield did inform you about my role here, did she not?"

Calming himself before answering. Damien stares at Benjamin: looking for any sign he could be lying.

"Of course, Benjamin, she did mention you disposed of the flowers and performed other duties on the property. If I may ask, would you be willing to continue doing so for Maddison Graves?"

"I am willing to continue, Although you are incorrect in your assumption, I do not dispose of the flowers as you are suggesting, Mr. Steele."

"Please Benjamin, call me Damien, Mr. Steele is too personal. My apologies for assuming incorrectly your role here and thank you for staying on, Of course if you are concerned about compensation, we will match anything Miss Lancefield is paying you."

"I do not get paid to do this Damien. I must go now and distribute these flowers. I do not dispose of them."

Damien watched as Benjamin walked away from the steps around the side of the house and out of sight.

Thinking to himself. "That is a strange dude." Then Damien turns to lock the door with the key and replacing it under the yellow planter.

Driving back to Maddison's house he reflects on Annette's request.

"I have your word, do I not?"

WATER

Damien knows this house is a special place. It will be difficult to prove otherwise. To himself he says,

"I do not believe this "Water" faucet thing is truly real."

Although he admits, it provides hope to people who need their spirits lifted. His thoughts continue deliberating back and forth whether or not he could make money on this escapade.

For Maddisson's sake he would go along with the ruse that the "water" has healing properties until he can prove otherwise.

Then he will have to deal with Maddison and any evidence he produces. Until then he will go along with the game as it is played.

Parking the car in Maddison's garage. He takes a deep breath before entering the house to discuss his findings. He has concluded there is no reason to discuss the faucet or the water with Maddison unless she brings it up.

A Long Talk

Damien finds his Maddison on the sofa in the living room reading a book titled. "Do-it-yourself home remodeling." He hears the soft tones of jazz music emanating from the built-in speakers throughout the house. She has no clue Damien has walked in.

Walking around behind the sofa he cannot resist the urge to scare her by tugging on a strand of her black hair.

Frantically she jumps up from her lounging position. Swiftly turns to locate what she assumed to be a bug in her hair; Instinctively without thinking she throws her book at Damien then yells.

"What are you doing? You scared me to death. I thought I had a spider on me."

"Sorry, I could not resist the temptation. You were engrossed in reading the book you did not notice I walked in the room."

Damien reaches down to retrieve the novel from the floor and looks at the cover.

"Nice! I am glad to see you are reading this book. That place will need a lot of repairs."

"My apologies for throwing the book at you, "D." Come around here and sit with me so we can discuss our options."

"I must say I like the sound of "our options."

"Sit down and listen for a minute. I have some ideas for us to consider."

Damien finds his way around to the front of the sofa and while sitting he hands off the book to Maddison.

"I am all ears my love."

159

WATER

Maddison begins with her thoughts on where to begin repairing the structure of the home. It needs a new roof, The front Porte Cochere needs rotting wood removed and replaced, not to mention new windows were first on her list of items. The list she shared with Damien was a long one.

Damien matched his thoughts on the construction and the timing of completion while conveying they should not attempt to move in until most of the work is completed. Expressing his concerns for their health during the phases of construction. Emphasizing the dust and debris would make it a hazard to breath in any mold or dust aggravated while the contractor is demolishing and rebuilding.

"You also remember we are getting married next month. You did not forget about that small detail have you?"

"Of course not. All of those plans have been in place for months now. Do not worry about that detail. I am looking forward to and planning on being Mrs. Damien Steele."

"That is a relief and puts a smile on my face."

"Ok, back to the house now."

"So quickly we move on from discussing us."

"Pay attention Damien."

"Yes my love."

{6:00PM Maddison's home}

Damien refrains from mentioning his meeting with Annette.

When the marathon discussion has concluded with both Maddison and Damien exhausted from their discussion while having mild differences in opinion of how the house should look after construction is completed.

Damien wants the basement for a man cave then concedes after Maddison denies his motion to proceed. He then breaks away from his conviction of not discussing anything in the basement and confesses he wants to remove the faucet.

161

Maddison walks into the kitchen to cool off. Opens the refrigerator and declares.

"Looks like we are going out for dinner tonight. There is nothing in this fridge but coffee."

"Say no more. I have the keys in my hand. What is your pleasure tonight steak, pizza or sushi?"

"Pizza."

Damien knew the answer to his question before he posed it to her. But instead of mentioning he had pizza pie earlier. He decides it was not in his interest to mention his meeting with Annette.

"I know just the place where they make true Italian pies from scratch. I will take you to Denino's on Staten Island."

"I love how you can make decisions for us. It is your best qualities as a man."

"Does this mean?"

162

"Rewards are duly earned my love."

"Yippee."

{7:00 PM Denino's Pizzeria & Tavern}

Damien and Maddison are now finished consuming the large meatball pizza with pineapple on one half for Maddison when they noticed a young girl had walked up to their table. Turning their heads Maddison asks.

"Can I help you miss?"

Nervously fiddling with her hands in front of her she calmly replies.

"It is about my brother."

"What about your brother?" Maddison asks.

"He has some problems with his speech. No doctor or speech therapist has

163

been able to help him I was wondering if he could come to the house and drink the "water?"

Maddison and Damien are taken back by the young girl's request. The house has not been fully transferred to them yet. Damien and Maddison take a quick look at each other. Damien turns to address her. Young lady we have not taken over completely. We literally signed the papers yesterday and we have thirty days before it is finalized and we begin renovations.

Maddison speaks up to ask the young girl.

.

"How did you know it was us who bought the Lancefield's home?"

"Ma'am everyone knows."

The words were spoken as the young lady turns to point out with a hand gesture. Everyone in the Pizzeria was staring at them.

Every customer, every waitstaff, even the cooks behind the counter standing or sitting had their eyes on the two of them.

164

WATER

When the young girls' voice broke their trance.

"Can you help my brother? Please, I believe all he has to do is drink the "water" from the faucet in the basement."

Maddison and Damien once again look at each other with bewilderment. Damien uses his lips to form soundless words to Maddison.

"What do we do?"

While turning to address the girl Maddison reaches out to hold her nervous hands with hers. Immediately her hands are calmed from Maddison's touch, She replies.

"Yes, yes of course we will allow your brother to drink from the faucet. I am sure he will need a number of sessions before he is healed. Can you bring him by tomorrow morning, say 9:00 am,

"Yes, I will meet you there at the house."

WATER

The young girl was crying tears of joy. She found the people who bought the house. She believes her younger brother would finally be cured of his speech patterns.

Maddison and Damien are on the way home when Damien asks.

"Are you going to call Annette to help you with this?"

"I need to Damien. I have never done this. It just might be my calling."

"May be Maddison, you never know."

{7:00AM Maddison's Home}

Maddison leaves her bedroom after getting dressed for her meeting with the young girl she encountered at the Pizza place.

Damien is already in her kitchen preparing their morning coffee.

WATER

"My darling you did not need to come here this early to make my coffee. This is so sweet and kind of you. You know how to make me love you."

"Thank you for the compliment. I like making coffee here."

"Why is that my love, you can't get enough of me?"

"Yes, although you have a better coffee maker than I do and your water filter is better than mine. So, are you meeting the young girl and her brother?"

"Yes at nine o'clock, why do you ask?"

"Honestly, I am still a bit skeptical of all this. It looks like a scheme Annette, and her family have been playing on people and you. This "water" from a basement faucet. How is it possible to heal people?"

"Damien, It is in the powers that be, I am unable to grasp how or why people come to that house requesting to drink from the faucet, but they are still coming."

"Last night was very weird. How do you think that young girl knew we were in that restaurant and that we were the new owners of the Lancefield home?"

WATER

"I do not know the answer to your question Damien, and I do not believe you do either."

"You know what I think, Annette has something to hide. We are not being told everything."

"Well, I think you just do not believe in the "water." I experienced it, I believe in it."

"We are at odds with our opinions, and I do not want it to come between us. I do not trust her and this scam. We will eventually get discovered."

"Damien."

"What now Maddison?"

"Enough for now before it drives you crazy and a wedge between us. I am leaving to meet that young lady now. Goodbye."

{9:00AM The Lancefield house}

WATER

On the top of the hour Maddison and Annette watch her new friend leading a younger boy up the stone walkway to meet them. Maddison is the first to address the two children that have approached the house.

"Please come inside. I am sorry. I did not get your name yesterday at the Pizza place."

"I am "Sam" short for Samantha, and this is my brother Danny. Can he drink the water now?"

"Yes of course. Follow me. By the way, Sam this is Annette Lancefield."

"I know who she is. Where is the faucet?"

Annette looks at the young boy to ask.

"Do you understand how to take directions?"

Nodding his head in agreement he attempts to form the word yes, it sounds like yeth.

WATER

Maddison listens as Annette explains in detail what the he is to do when he gets in the basement.

"Stand in front of the faucet. If the water flows you are to drink as much of it as you can. When it stops flowing you come back upstairs."

Maddison closes the door behind him as he descends the steps. They now wait for his return. It is Maddison's first time helping someone. She is uneasy with this procedure but otherwise happy to help the young girl who believes her brother would benefit from the power of the "water."

She turns to engage in conversation with Sam.

"How old are you Sam?"

"I just turned thirteen, when will my brother start getting better?"

Maddison looks towards Annette for guidance when she informs Maddison.

"She asked you, not me."

WATER

Maddison was unsure what her response should be as Annette left it squarely in her hands to find the right answer.

"Sam, your brother will need a few more trips down those steps. You will see an improvement each time he comes, I promise you. In order for the "water" to help. You have to be a believer also."

Maddison again looks at Annette for approval. A nod of her head and a faint smile appearing on her face. It was just enough to acknowledge she passed muster.

A faint knock on the door. Maddison sweeps past Annette to open the heavy wooden basement door allowing Danny to navigate the last step. Sam rushes to his side embracing him with a strong hug then takes his hand to lead him to the front door for their return trip home. Annette and Maddison following close behind them onto the porch. When they reach the stone walkway Maddison says.

"Good-bye, come back tomorrow at the same time if you wish."

Danny turns away from his sister and replies with perfect formation of his words.

171

"Thank-you, we will return tomorrow."

Maddison covered her mouth with her hand with disbelief. They boy spoke the words perfectly.

"Annette, did you hear that boy?"

"Yes, Maddison. Now you have a story of your own to tell the next generation."

{12:30PM Maddison's house}

Maddison stops the car with a screech in the garage. Jumps out and runs inside into the waiting arms of Damien.

"It worked, "D," The boy drank the water and spoke perfectly on his way out the door to go home. IT WORKED! Do

172

you believe me, now do you believe in the power of the "water?"

Maddison was soaking Damiens shirt with tears of joy. Waiting for Damien to acknowledge her accomplishment. When he did not immediately respond. She let go of him and stepped back looking him in the eyes with a questionable look on her face. She yearned for Damiens support and approval.

"Ok "D." Do you think I am crazy for believing in what, I experienced today?"

"Maddison, my Maddison. I believe in what you believe. I am here for you, by your side on this journey. We are in this together. All I ask from you is this. Can you have faith in me that sometimes, I will be skeptical and other times a believer. That is who I am."

"Ok, for now, I will accept that about you."

"Now My love. Can you help me understand what happened today? I am extremely nervous at the moment. Let's sit down. I will share the details of the meeting with you."

Damien agreed as the two reclined to the sofa. Maddison opened up relaying the experience with great detail. When she was finished she asked Damien to go home. She needed her time to reflect on today's event by herself in her own way.

Damien agreed he would go home. But instead.

He headed to the Lancefield house.

WATER

Back at the scene

{1:45PM Lancefield home.}

Damien takes large strides on the stones to the Porte Cochere. Leaping up from the first step missing the second and lands squarely on the wood decking, directly at the front door. Reaching for the handle without thinking to get the key, the handle turns and the door opens.

Taking a moment standing in the framework that secures the door. He ponders, "where should I start looking this time."

Damien heads to the basement to look for a hidden compartment. Maybe there is someone hiding in plain sight down there. He reaches for the light switch, missing a step and stumbles once before catching his balance.

Swiftly he descends while frantically searching the four walls for a hidden compartment. His mind wanders in thought.

"I have seen something like this on one of those scary late night TV shows."

Not enough light from the single bulb he wishes he had a flashlight. Looking up at the ceiling he spots the cellar's exterior bulkhead doors angling out to the outside. Although the old wooden stairs leading up to them had been removed he decides to relocate himself outside to take a look to see if it they could possibly have been of use as an advantage point to turn on the "water."

Damien exits the basement quickly with large strides. He is up and out the basement door heading out the back door from the kitchen. Now down three steps and swiftly turns the corner of the house. There in the overgrowth of landscaping he can barely manage to make out the slanted form of the cellar doors. It was obvious to him; they had not been cleaned off or opened in several years.

Damien's hopes now dashed. He begins to search the side of the house along with every inch of the yard for any sign that may shed some truth to his theory. That this place is a scam. Slowing down he remembers his promise to Annette and what it would do to this place.

If that thought wasn't enough, what would it do to his Maddison? She is now deep in her belief Annette has been truthful, and this place is the real deal.

Thinking out loud again he says to himself. I have to know for myself, if not anything else, "I" have to know the truth."

Damien is now slightly out of breath, he walks the perimeter of the property aligned with the hedgerow that is some ten feet tall, sectioning off the neighbors' houses from what is happening on this side of it. He spots a thin opening just large enough for the thin frame of Benjamin to slip through.

Damien turns his body sideways sucking in his chest as he slips thru into what appears to be Bennys' adjacent back yard. He locks eye contact onto the house, now catching his breath after holding it while traversing the hedge. He hears the voice again.

May I help You?"

Damien thrusts away from the hedge falling on to his backside trying to flee from what has just startled him.

Recovering from his fall he dusts himself off. It is Benjamin who was standing a few feet from him on the other side of the hedge row. When he asked the question that sent Damien into a tailspin.

Damien yells out:

"You idiot! You scared he crap out of me."

"My apologies Mr. Steele but in my defense I was here first trimming my side of the hedge. I have trimmers in my hands to prove my case."

"I know you are a damn lawyer; you do not have to talk in lawyer terminology. I am not stupid."

"Then may I ask why you've chosen to trespass onto my property sir?"

WATER

"Do not challenge or try to debate me about my motive, Benny. What I am looking for does not concern you at the moment. Now if you do not mind I will be leaving your property."

"Excellent idea Mr. Steele."

Damien turns away from Benjamin keeping an eye on him as he turns sideways to slip back onto the Lancefield side of the hedge. As he makes his way thru, his right shoe catches something sticking out of the ground. He falls face first into the grass.

"What was that? Yelling out again at Benjamin. Did, you trip me Benny?"

Benjamin answers him from the other side of the fence.

"I forgot to mention to watch out for the water valve, I use to water the lawn."

Damien looks down. At the edge of the hedge is a double valve with a faucet on one end. The four-spoke handle looks identical to the faucet on the basement wall.

WATER

Making a mental note he walks away refraining to say anything more to Benjamin who is now parting the hedge with his hands to watch Damiens' backside thru the leaves of the hedge as he shamefully walks away.

Damien walks to his car. Standing at the driver's door he begins to brush off the remaining grass and dirt from his shirt, pants and hair. Checks his nose. It is not broken although it is bruised. He now worries about his pride and how to regain the respect he has lost with Benjamin.

Now starting the car, he checks his face in the rear-view mirror, then turns up the radio to his favorite soul station, slams the shifter in gear, pressing the gas pedal igniting the fuel and air mixture. The rear tires spin, screeching a loud noise while producing burnt smoke as the car leaves its parking spot.

Damien is headed home to his house. Maddison must never know he was here.

Stripping down he enters the walk-in shower to rinse of the remaining residue from his falls. The warm water flowed from the showerhead as grit and sandy particles were being washed off.

WATER

Lowering his head he watched the water carry the stained soap from his hair and body disappear from his view down the drain.

His mind is in a quandary. Is it really the power of the "water" that heals people or a higher belief than he is not comprehending. Damien relates the water that is flowing over him, cleansing him of dirt to the "water" from the faucet cleansing the people of their problems. In essence healing them from ailments and disease.

He ponders the situation he and Maddison are inheriting from the purchase. How is this happening and why the Lancefield house? The remaining question he has for himself "stills" him in the shower. What about the Spirit Annette mentioned at lunch?

Raising his head, then tilting it backward allowing the water from the showerhead to hit him directly on his face. Reaching for the showers valve he shuts off the flow raining down on him.

The answer hits like a brick. He figured out how the water flows from the faucet in the basement. While someone is standing in front of it. What does he ask

182

himself now? The only caveat stopping him from telling Maddison is his pact with Annette.

It overpowers his thoughts.

He can never tell anyone. Not even his beloved Maddison.

{4:45AM Damien's home.}

Lying in bed awake, unable to rest himself. Damien rolls over to turn on the lamp on his nightstand next to his bed. Exiting the warmth of his comforter. He grabs his robe and heads for the kitchen to open the refrigerator.

Grabbing a cold beer then placing it back on the shelf and selecting the orange juice instead. In lieu of a glass, he man drinks it straight from the container.

Sitting down at the kitchen table he begins a deliberation with himself. How do

WATER

WATER

I keep this from Maddison?" Better yet how do I convince her this activity has been a charade from the beginning. A "SPIRIT" he asks himself.

Knowing full well the answer to that question will be tricky to pull off. But maybe just maybe he can keep the ruse in place. He will need to have the one and only accomplice working with him.

The one- and only-man Annette has employed to pull this off must be on board with him. That will enable this hustle to continue for years to come. He would not have to tell Maddison so quickly, as he concludes she will eventually figure it out on her own and he will not be the bearer of the unwelcome news.

Keeping the secret from Maddison will be his greatest challenge. Damien raises the jug in the air with his arm then turns up the jug of orange juice to his lips and swallows a mouthful. It was his way of confirming his plan to himself. The same scenario that plays out with cocktail glasses clinking between friends at the club.

With this plan, his mind is at ease, it is time to rest now. Returning to his bed, he lays his head on the double king size soft pillows and falls asleep.

{9:50 AM The next morning.}

Damien's phone rings waking him up. Still half-asleep Damien reaches for the receiver. It is Maddison.

"Oh, my darling, are you ok?"

"Yes, why do you ask Maddison?"

"Damien, my love, do you know what time it is?"

"No."

"It is near ten O'clock. I have been worried about you. You are not here making my coffee and breakfast. I came downstairs thinking you were here, you are not here! I thought something happened to you."

"Maddison, I am fine, I just had a little trouble sleeping last night. I am deeply sorry, but I obviously overslept."

WATER

"Are you sick? Can I bring you something? Never mind answering, I am already in the car on the way to you."

Before Damien could call off Maddison she hung up. Damien rises and dresses himself. Walking out to his living room, Maddison bursts thru his garage door and leaps into his arms.

"Don't scare me like that ever again Damien, I was extremely worried about you."

"My apologies for breaking our morning protocol, it was not intentional."

"Where did you go yesterday after you left my house? You always call to say good night. You did not do that either."

Damien was in the hot seat. Three choices quickly run thru his head. Tell her where he went, produce a diversion or tell her a lie.

{10:25AM The diversion.}

"Hey Maddie, what do you say, I treat you to breakfast at the local diner this morning?"

"Ok, I am hungry. And I need my coffee since you were not there to make it for me."

"I will grab my keys meet you in the garage in five."

{10:50AM The Diner.}

"I know what you like to eat for breakfast. Would you like me to order for you?"

"Yes you may my love. By the way, don't think I know you used this breakfast date as a diversion to keep from answering my question. I will forgive you for not wanting to answer. I am not dumb nor or blonde."

"Thank you Maddison."

"One more thing Mr. Steele."

WATER

"Anything Maddie."

Maddison explodes on Damien.

"DO NOT call me MADDIE! Ever again. You know my uncle called me that and hearing it reminds me of him."

"Yes Maddison."

"Now, tell this waitress what we will be eating, she is waiting on you."

Damien takes her advice in jest and then orders eggs benedict for the both of them, with coffee in hand, Damien smiles at Maddison as she chooses to make direct eye contact with him. He watches as Maddison presents a huge smile while saying.

"I love you."

Breakfast is now served.

While eating Damien asks if she is to meet with the young girl and her brother again today."

WATER

"Oh, yes. Thank you for reminding me. I need to finish and get over there soon. They are coming around noon today."

"Would you like me to drive you there after we are finished?"

"Yes. Then you can experience the miracle of the "water" together with me."

"Say no more. I am your chauffeur."

Damien wishes he could just tell her right then and there how he feels and what he knows. He cannot, it is too early to confess what he "suspects" is happening and how this show will end. But he cannot bear to shatter the image she has of the show. It is obvious to him she is deeply committed at this point.

The time is not now; he cannot change her belief in the power the "water" has to change someone or even heal them.

{11:59AM The Lancefield house.}

WATER

Danien stops the car in front of the house repeating the scenario of how he will expose Annette and her accomplice. Just as he figured Annette was already on the portico awaiting Maddison's arrival.

Like clockwork they are standing together watching the little girl march her brother up the stone walkway and enter the house.

Annette leads the way with Maddison and the two young innocent children to the basement doorway. In case he forgot, Danny is again given the same instructions before he descends into the basement. Maddison stands as sentinel, beaming with joy. The miracle she came to see makes her day.

Damien watches diligently with his skepticism kept to himself. The door closes behind Danny. He is watching Annette make her move to the kitchen window to adjust the small curtains suppressing the light in the room. She opens them then closes them a fleeting time later.

Maddison has her eyes trained on the wooden basement door, Unaware of the signal Annette had just given Benjamin awaiting outside at the hedgerow.

WATER

It played out just as Damien figured it would. Playing it as cool as he could. He let the game continue. Annette catches a glimpse of Damien looking at her. She smiles and readjusts the curtains once more, then walks to the door to greet Danny emerging from the basement.

Samantha takes his hand leading him out the front door, Maddison right behind them to say good-bye.

"I hope this is helping you Danny. I will be here tomorrow at the same time if you need to come one more time."

His reply is all Madison needed to confirm the "water is making a difference in his speech when he replies with precise pronunciation.

"Thank Miss Graves, I will be back tomorrow."

Maddison almost loses control to stand. Her knees buckle, she sheds a tear and turns to Damien."

191

WATER

"Damien, did you hear him? He can speak without stuttering. He life is changing before our eyes. Do you believe me now? The "water is healing him. Can you see it? You can definitely hear it from him?"

Annette stands behind Maddison with her hands together in front of her. She keeps her silence as Maddison confronts Damien with her revelation. She winks at Damien then replies to Maddison directly.

"I am sure he has a lot on his mind right now my dear Maddison. This may be too much for him to accept at the moment. I suggest the two of you take some time together for a few days, I can handle the house. I believe you two are getting married next week, are you not?"

"Why, yes we are. I had almost forgotten about it with buying this house. It is all I have been thinking about lately."

Damien is miffed at Maddison's acknowledgement. His feelings are ruffled and walks away from the two women who share parting comments.

WATER

Damien awaits for his bride to be at the car's passenger door. Once securing his bride to be inside the car, he walks around to enter the driver's seat, starts the car without saying a word to Maddison and begins their journey back to his house where she left her car.

Maddison senses his mood while they are traveling. She waits until he parks the car in his garage, then reaches over to grasp his hand. He instantly stops and looks at her. He knows her well. She has something to say and he should listen.

"I am sorry if my statement hurt your feelings back at the Lancefield house. I want you to know. Our marriage together is the most magnificent thing we can achieve together. I love that you've asked me to be your wife and Damien; I would not want to marry anyone else."

"Thank you Maddie, OOOPS! Maddison."

"I am gonna hurt you one day, Damien Steele."

"Hmmmm. I might like that."

"Yea, me too, now give me a kiss, then we can go inside and finish what we have started here in this garage."

"Game on! Maddison."

"You are such a man, get in the house."

Wedding Bells

{6:00PM Saturday afternoon.}

Maddison Graves is in full wedding gown. Standing in front of a large mirror. Her bridesmaids surround her. The chatter is annoying; all girl talk that contains the subject of men.

Silently, she wishes her mother could be here to give her advice. Not only for today but for her future as Mrs. Damien Steele.

Her father never re-married and she never asked him why, just assumed he could never find another woman to complete him like the mother she never knew. In silence her tears flow from her eyes as she remembers the man that gave up every extracurricular activity just to ensure she had a parent attending every event in her life to support her.

Maddison takes in one more look at herself in the mirror, wiping the tears with a napkin, her reflection resembles the pictures of her mother when she married her dad. She realizes she definitely has her mother's figure as the dress fits perfectly. Another gracious gift from her father, keeping it all these years just for this day.

Cynthia Steele, Damien's mother filled in as her surrogate mother and her closest female ally over the years. She walks up and stands close to Maddison, observing her movements and pondering thoughts. A lite touch from her hand touches Maddison's shoulder.

"Maddison, honey, are you ready for this? You look amazing. I sometimes wish you were my daughter."

WATER

Her kind words turn into an embrace. They release as the knock on the door signals the music is playing. They need to leave the room. It is time to marry her son.

{8:15Pm The reception.}

Damien and Maddison enter the large indoor venue. The "DJ" hands over the microphone as the two are introduced as Mr. and Mrs. Damien Steele.

It will be a few hours later before they get back together and have their first dance as husband and wife. The room is silent except for the song they selected for this day. All eyes are on them until the end when the roar of cheers and more well wishes pulls them apart again.

{12:10AM midnight.}

Damien and Maddison must now leave the festivities. A large limousine is waiting outside loaded with their luggage for a week in the Caribbean. Compliments of Damiens' father and mother. It was a family tradition to honeymoon there and to have family vacations in the timeshare they have owned for years.

{9:00AM two days after arrival.}

Maddison wakes up and opens the blackout curtains. The sun has risen, and the light is hurting Damiens eyes as he tries to wake up. Maddison turns around to look at her man still lying in bed. Damien turns on his side to view his wife. He has a smile on his face.

She asks.

"Are you really that happy we are finally married my love?"

"Yes I am and I am excited to see your body framed against the sunlight coming in thru those windows."

"Stop it "D" we have been in bed for a day and a half. Let's go walk on the beach today. I want to find some shells to take home as a reminder of our honeymoon and I am starving. I've never gone this long without eating."

"Yes, I agree eating solid food is on my agenda as well. Can we eat first at the

197

restaurant downstairs to regain enough energy for a walk?"

"Absolutely, now get out of bed and quit staring at me. We both need a shower."

"That is hard to do Maddison. You are the most beautiful woman I have ever married."

His remarks stop her from heading into the shower room. She turns to respond.

"I better be the only woman you've ever married. Mr. Steele."

"I will never tell."

"Shut up, get in the shower with me."

"Coming my darling."

Out of the shower Maddison takes some time to get herself publicly presentable. When Damien comes close to Maddison still sitting at the Vanity finishing up her makeup.

WATER

"Maddison we are at the beach, let's go eat."

"Get used to it big boy. This is what you married. Ok, I am done let's go."

{Seven days later, 10:25AM LaGuardia Airport.}

Departing the Caribbean their flight lands, they are now back home. Damien and Maddison head to the baggage retrieval area.

There is a man next to the turnstile holding up a sign that reads. "Mr. and Mrs. Steele."

Another limo driver is there to take them home. Connecting with him, he offers to grab their luggage while he points to the awaiting limousine just outside the revolving glass door.

Tired from the trip Damien takes Madisons' hand and leads her outside, There another man in a suit opens the vehicles door and ushers them inside. A pleasant voice says, "Make yourself comfortable, We will have you home shortly. Hope you had a great honeymoon."

Maddison enters first with Damien following. Sitting in the comfortable bench seat Maddison leans over and rests her head on Damiens' shoulder.

She speaks softly to Damien.

"Remind me to contact your mother tomorrow to thank her for the Limo ride."

"She would love to hear from you. And when you "do" speak with her. Tell her about the house you bought us."

"That is a great idea "D."

"Maddison."

"Yes."

"How come you can refer to me as "D," but I cannot use Maddie for you?"

"You were my boyfriend until now. If you want, you can use Maddie from now on."

"You amaze me with your analytics. I prefer to use Maddison most of the time, "unless" I am mad at you. I love you more."

200

Maddison curls up closer to Damien, She sniffles and reaches for a tissue from the door pocket of the limousine.

"Did you catch a cold in the Caribbean?"

"I do not think this is a cold. My stomach is queasy also."

"You might have gotten the flu bug from one of our guests at the reception. It is about time for it to manifest in you after being exposed."

"I will be fine. Once we get some rest. You wore me out this past week."

"I was hoping."

"No Damien, I need time to recover."

"I will leave you alone then."

"You are such a man. I love you more."

{11:35PM Damiens home."}

WATER

Tired from traveling Mr. and Mrs. Damien Steele settle into bed together and curl up next to each other. Damien embraces his wife in his arms comforting her. When she starts a volley of sneezes. Damien jumps out of bed to retrieve a box of tissue.

"You are sick Maddison. I am taking you to the doctor tomorrow and do not say, "no thank you" because I will not accept it."

"Ok, I like how you demand to take care of me. Thank you for the tissues. Now, come back to bed. We will see how I feel in the morning, Maybe I need to go into the basement and drink some of the magical "water.""

Damien hears his wife but remains silent, choosing not to answer or provide feedback to her statement. Instead, he crawls under the covers, kisses her on the forehead and continues to embrace the love of his life.

{9:00AM The sun's rays.}

WATER

Damien is the first out of bed, letting Maddison sleep longer. He walks into the kitchen to make coffee.

The first cup is consumed when he reads the morning news on his laptop. Nothing amazing is happening in the world, just the standard fake headlines. He looks at the clock on the wall. It is now 11:00 Am. Maddison is still in bed. Deciding he needs to check on her then refrains as he hears her stirring in the bathroom.

Damien gets a cup of coffee ready for her arrival.

Maddison sits down across from her husband. Forming a smile while feeling puny is like climbing Everest, but she manages one for him.

"I see you are not feeling well my dear. I will call the doctor to see if he can fit you in today."

"Please no "D." I am ok. I believe. It was the Oysters I ate the day we left. My stomach will recover. We do not need to spend money on a doctor's visit. I promise there is nothing he can do about this that Pepto Bismol won't fix."

203

WATER

"Ok, Maddie. Have it your way."

"Do not be mad at me. I know my body."

"How do you know I am mad at you?"

"You called me Maddie."

"Touché."

"Go do some work before your father terminates you. You have not been into the office in weeks."

"I have been working remotely. Checking the emails and following up on orders. Dad is happy."

"Alright then. Make me some chicken soup."

Maddison is now sipping on the soup as Damien retreats to his study to check on work. He makes a few phone calls with one to his father.

"Hey Dad, how are things, I have been checking emails and making the orders remotely, Did that client sign the insurance documents I sent to him? I don't have confirmation yet."

"Yes he did, we sent out the final paperwork to him this morning. The delivery status has not been updated yet.

So, I hear you and Maddison bought a house."

"Yes, Maddison actually bought it for the two of us to live in. It needs some work."

"I hear your mother talking to Maddison in the other room now. They are planning to get together to look at it tomorrow morning."

"I am sure mom will be surprised at what she sees."

"I will leave it at that son. Talk to you later, I have to deal with work issues at the moment."

{10:00AM The Lancefield home.}

The two pull into a parking spot in front of the old house.

WATER

"Thanks for picking me up and driving us here Cynthia. I have not been feeling my best since our honeymoon."

"My pleasure Maddison, this will give us girls some time together. Let's go inside and you can show me around. It is a lovely house you've purchased. I can't wait to see what changes you have in mind."

Maddison opens the front door and immediately becomes nauseated. Without saying a word, she runs to one of the bathrooms to throw up in the toilet. Damien's mother is right behind her.

As she waits for Maddison to finish, she realizes Maddison's condition.

"My dear Maddison, you are with child."

"What?"

Maddison stands erect and looks at her mother-in-law.

"Mom, I do not think so, but why do you make such an assumption?"

206

WATER

"My dear Maddison, I have been in this same situation. The signs are there. And I am so happy for the two of you."

Maddison is speechless. Knowing full well the cost to her if she tries to carry this baby to full term. She begins to turn pale, almost fainting.

"Mom, I need to sit down."

"Come we can sit on the front porch, and you can tell me about the house from there."

Maddison agrees but before she can leave the bathroom she empties her stomach one more time.

The two women are now on the front porch having a pleasant discussion of the house and it has a history of helping people who come from all over the country, further explaining the power of the "water."

"I do not feel like getting up but you can walk in the main living room and see the photos of all the people this place has helped over the years."

"I will see it another time. Right now, I think I should take you to my OBGYN doctor."

Maddison is still in denial but succumbs to her mother-in-law's request.

"Ok, I will go with you. But promise me you will not say anything to your son. That will be my right as his wife to do so."

"You have my word Maddie."

"Now I know where he gets that from."

"Get what?"

"Never mind, mom."

"Maddison, I have always wanted a daughter."

"Well, You are stuck with me now."

"I accept that. Now get in the car."

Maddison and Cynthia step out of the house onto the porch. Benjamin is recovering several bouquets of flowers left on the steps. Greetings and introductions follow when Maddison's stomach begins to churn again.

208

WATER

"Excuse me mom I have to step back inside for a moment, I need a drink of water from the basement, please feel free to chat with Benny. I will return shortly."

Maddison leaves the two to get acquainted. Cynthia takes a step down from the porch when Benjamin hears Maddison's request for "water." He replies.

"Excuse me ma'am, I must attend to something at the back of the house."

Disappearing to the hedgerow as Maddison is now facing the faucet. The "water" flows and she drinks. A vibrance engulfs her, she believes the water is calming her stomach. Fully convinced she is feeling better she steps outside to greet her Mother-in-law.

"All good now mom, let's go."

Cynthia asks; "What is with the "water from the basement?"

Time for Believing

{10:00AM 6 weeks later. The Lancefield home}

Maddie and Annette have closed on the house. Damien meets with Annette and Benjamin at the house to discuss how they should continue providing the "water" to the many people who seek its healing properties.

"Let me ask you this question Annette. Do you unequivocally believe in the "water" as a powerful healing source when ingested?"

"Yes, I do. I have seen how it has effected many people. I know it is strange to you, how we deliver it when someone is

210

in front of the faucet, but that "water" heals the sick. I am convinced of it. In time, Mr. Steele, you too will be convinced as you experience the miracles that come before you. These experiences will change your perspective of its power."

Still Skeptical Damien jokingly asks.

"Another question Annette. Should we tell people this is "Holy Water or Spiritual Water?"

"I do not recommend referencing the "water" to anyone in such a manner. As people come to you, you will have to ask questions regarding their beliefs. You will learn who has a real problem or who is here as a fake. Stay clear of them. The spirit controls the water. It knows who is not of faith. And will not let the water flow even though the valve is turned on."

"Now we are going back to where I have doubts of the water's healing properties. I need to know the truth Annette. Does this "water" actually have the ability to heal the sick? You keep mentioning the spirit knows who is real and who is fake. So, if you "believe" someone

211

is a fake, do you give Benjamin a different "signal," to not turn on the valve?"

Shaking her head Annette stood back and crossed her arms.

"My dear Mr. Steele, it is the "SPIRIT'S" choice to appear from the faucet in the form of the "water." All we do is give it the path to flow. It is not of our doing whether it comes out of the faucet. It will only flow for the true believer."

With Annettes' last statement Damien took a moment to digest her words.

"Is that why it will not flow for me, even though you instructed Benjamin to turn on the valve?"

"Correct Mr. Steele."

"Can you prove it to me?"

"Of course. You can watch thru the window and Benjamin will turn on the valve. Then you can go down in the basement and stand in front of the faucet. You can prove it to yourself."

WATER

Damien took Annette up on her offer. After watching Benjamin turn on the outside valve he went downstairs to try the faucet again. Just as before, he faucet was dry. His skepticism prevented the flow.

Benjamin walked into the kitchen's back door as Damien appeared from the basement doorway.

"You two are tricky. You turned off the "water" when I went down there. Didn't you?"

Benjamin had enough of Damiens' skepticism. He steps forward to confront him.

"Mr. STEELE! I take exception to your accusation. That water is on. Miss Lancefield's' grandfather discovered the water coming out of the ground years ago. It is a natural spring. No electric pump brings it up into this house. I am living proof the "water" flows, and it healed me. I am a true believer with unquestionable faith. Let me prove it to you.

"How do you plan to do that Benny."

"I will go down in the basement right now and wet my hands with the water and return up here to you. I have never failed to extract water from the faucet."

"If you can do that while I watch the hedgerow from the window I will be closer to believing in all of this you say is true."

Benjamin turned to walk thru the basement doorway. Before he took one step into the basement he turned to make sure Damien was looking out the window, then descended to the faucet.

Standing before the faucet. He waited. Nothing appeared. He questioned himself and his faith. He could not figure out why the delay is happening. He stands before the faucet a little longer.

"Waiting."

Damien yells down thru the open doorway.

"Any "water" yet, Benny?"

Benjamin thinks, then realizes the door is open. The spirit knows this. He yells up to Annette.

"Annette, close the door."

214

WATER

Annette closes the door on Benjamin's request. He is now alone with the faucet. He lowers his head, cupping his hands together, placing them under the faucet.

He is rewarded with the healing liquid flowing from the faucet he once used to heal his own problems. Holding his hands and fingers tightly together he walks up the stairs and asks thru the door for it to be opened.

Damien walks to the doors edge. He sees the "water" in Benjamins' hands.

"Here is your proof! Mr. Steele. You are welcome to drink the "water" from my hands. I "promise" you will be changed forever."

Damien stood motionless, staring at the liquid in Benjamins hands. It was clearer than any water he had ever seen. He can see every line in the hands as he tightly cupped the water to prevent it from spilling. Damien is now tempted to lower his head to drink from Benjamins' hands.

215

WATER

Before he could take a sip. The spirit would not have it. The water vanished before his eyes. Benjamins' hands were now dry with no trace of the liquid ever being present.

"Do you believe us now Mr. Steele? It is not that we turn it on as a hoax to people This is not a a magical trick.

We turn it on for the believers and it is up to the "spirit" to appear before the faithful. It, choses who to appear for and who it "chooses" to heal. Obviously, it does not choose you at this time."

Damien is speechless from the words so eloquently spoken from Benjamin. Still somewhat skeptical he admits to the two in front of him.

"I am close, although I need more proof this stuff actually works on someone. It would be nice if I could experience it healing someone close to me. That way I would know it is the real thing, or it is not."

Annette responds to his statement.

"Damien Steele, That time will soon come for you. You will believe in due time."

WATER

Benjamin turns toward Damien before he leaves the house.

"If what you just experienced did not convince you then maybe you will never become a believer. I will leave now good-bye Mr. Steele."

"Thank you for your parting words Benjamin. Miss Lancefield, it is time for us to go our separate ways. I will handle the "water" and your spirit from now on. Thank you for your advice and direction. This has been a learning experience. I am assured if my wife needs any advice in the future, she will be in contact."

Annette leaves the house for the last time. But before she does she walks into the room of photographs.

"If you do not mind. I would like to take this one with me."

"Why that one, Is that little girl special to you?"

Annette removes the one picture, selected from the wall of hundreds of others. Partially obscured from other photos surrounding it. One wouldn't know it was there had she not reached for it specifically. Damien watches as she pauses to hold the photo staring at it for a moment then asks.

"Annette, will you tell me her story before you leave?"

"Yes, If you wish. This is Francene. The neighbor's little girl. She was ten years old when she was struck by a car in front of the house."

Annette is choking up while trying to tell the story. Damien senses her emotion.

"It is ok if this story disturbs you, You do not need to continue with the rest of the story."

"I am ok. I need to share it with you.'

"Please continue, I would love to hear her story."

The teenager had just received her driving permit. Being a teenager, she had her girlfriends in the car with her. All cackling on about boys and going to the Friday night football game.

WATER

It was getting dark; in those days, the cars did not have automatic sensors to turn on the lights. Francene was riding her bike home from a girlfriend's house on the next block over from ours."

Annette paused again. Tears flow from her eyes. Damien asks.

"This is difficult for you to talk about, isn't it?"

"The driver did not see her in the road. After she was hit, she was brought here to the house. I begged my father to get her to the faucet. It was too late. She had already passed. There was nothing my father or the "water" could do to bring her back."

Damien had no words to convey. Re-living the tragedy of that day troubled Annette for some reason.

"Did the police charge the driver of the car? I hope the family forgave the driver."

"No charges were filed. The police said it was an unavoidable accident."

WATER

Annette paused then looking up she said with tears in her eyes, "Her mother and father never forgave me."

Damien slumped his shoulders upon hearing Annette's final words. He ascertained the power of the "water" could not heal everyone. Damien embraced Annette with a comforting hug, then let her walk away from the house for the last time.

Before Damien could turn to lock up and drive home to his wife. An older man stepped up from the sidewalk nearly passing Annette as she once again avoided the mailbox.

Damien watched as the man grew closer to the steps of the portico. The man's head was down. Watching his feet as each step brings him closer to Damien. He wore a soiled hat although he was clean cut and somewhat attractive for an older man. He completes the short walk and reaches the base of the first step.

"May I help you with something sir? Do you need directions? I have a car; I can drive you to where you need to go if you are lost."

WATER

"The gentleman who had stopped at the end of the stones, looked up at Damien. Reaching up with a clean well-manicured hand he tilted his hat backwards to have a better view of the man standing three steps above him on the porch decking.

"My name is Earl Larson. Is this the place that has the "water? I learned about it from a friend. I was not sure which house it was. I parked down the street and walked here."

Damien Steel looked down from the top of the porch, dumfounded at what to do. His memory played back the words Annette told him to focus on if someone came to the house seeking the "water."

{Ask the questions first and never turn anyone away.}

Figuring this would be his first test of the "waters" power. He would know if there truly was a spirit in control of its flow.

"Mr. Larson, I am Damien Steele the new owner of the Lancefield home. My wife and I finalized the paperwork this week.

221

WATER

May I invite you to come sit on the porch with me and tell me your story before I direct you to the faucet? I need to be sure you are of faith sir or the "water" cannot help you."

Damien reaches out with his hand to help the gentleman up and into one of the rocking chairs.

"Now that we are alone here Mr. Larson. Please tell me what your needs are."

"Yes of course. I am a widower and have been looking for the right woman to replace my wife. I own and operate an automotive repair shop in the suburbs of New York. It produces a great income, although some customers cannot afford my services. Over the many years of doing business with the public you get a feel for who can afford a repair job. So, I do not mind helping them and never charge for the work I do for them. Charging for any advice is out of the question, which is free.

The younger people these days do not understand the number 18436572 that is embedded in my head. That is the firing order for a small block chevy engine.

I have instructed my kids when I pass on. They should place an SBC engine on my grave as my marker instead of a tombstone."

"Mr. Larson, I understand you have an excellent work ethic, but do you have a disease, or a physical problem the "water" can help you with?"

"My problem sir is this, I am lonely; My wife passed away five years ago. I have been searching since then for a suitable partner. Do you know how hard that is Mr. Steele?

Can the "water give me the strength and courage to find a descent mate? Or send me in the right direction. It would be nice if it could send me somebody."

"Mr. Larson, I am not sure I understand your request."

"It is simple son. I have worked all my life building and starting engines. Now, I need someone that can start my engine and keep it running. I have done enough for everyone I know, It is my turn. Can the "water" I have heard so much about help me?"

WATER

Damien thought for a minute on Mr. Larson's request when he realized the water was still on. This would be a first test, if the water flows from the faucet for this man then it has to be real.

"I think I can help you sir. Please follow me."

Damien leads Mr. Larson to the basement door. He gives him the same instructions Annette insisted he provide to everyone that attempts to drink from the faucet.

Mr. Larson enters the basement; He turns on the light as instructed and descends to the basement floor. Damien closes the heavy door behind him. Reaching the bottom step, he walks over and stands in front of the Faucet. Damien waits diligently upstairs for his return.

A knock on the door signals he is finished, and Damien turns the handle to open the door. There in all his glory was Mr. Larson, who is wet from head to toe.

Damien chuckles, then asks.

"Why sir, are you all wet. You were only supposed to get a drink from the faucet."

WATER

"I am sorry, It came out so fast, I tried to slow it down. In my attempt to stop it is sprayed all over me. Does this mean, I am going to find a really good woman?"

Damien had no words for him. Dismayed at what happened. He watched Mr. Larson simply turn away from him and exit the house with the biggest smile he had ever seen on a man.

{2:30PM Damiens home.}

Damien enters the house from the garage door after parking the car. Calling out Maddison's name. He gets no response. Looking inside and on the back deck for his wife Maddison. He steps into the bedroom to find his wife asleep in bed. Gently he crawls in beside her. She emits a soft moan as he cradles her in his arms, they both continue napping.

WATER

{6:15PM Damien awakens.}

"Honey, I am getting up to start dinner, Are you hungry?"

Maddison responds as she rolls over to look at her man.

"I am, what are you preparing for us, my handsome chef?"

"A salad for you and meat and potatoes for me."

"You are such a man."

"I know. You remind me of it quite often. Get out of bed sleepy head. You've been in that bed all day."

"I realize that. You wore me out on our fabulous honeymoon time."

"I bet, now get up and come in the kitchen and talk to me about the meeting today with Annette and Benjamin. Then I will tell you about Mr. Larson."

"Oh! Yes I almost forgot about that. Let me get a shower and I will be out there soon. By the way. Who is Mr. Larson?"

"I will explain all that. Are you are getting in the shower? Can I scrub your back?"

"Go start dinner Please."

"As you command my love."

227

Acceptance

{One month later 7:00AM start time.}

Damien yells out at Maddison.

"Are you coming. The contractors start early in the morning, and I am assured they are already there waiting on us to approve the construction."

Maddison walks past her husband with a large manila envelope stuffed with papers and a lunch cooler filled with drinks.

"What may I ask do you have in that cooler?"

WATER

"I thought it would be a kind gesture to provide a couple of soda pops for the workers."

"Maybe so, but I know there are more workers than drinks you have in that cooler. Come along darling lets go."

"If you are right Mr. know it all, we can drink them."

The two proud owners drive to their new home. Turning the corner Maddison understands what her husband was conveying to her. There in front of the house were several different trucks adorned with their individual business signs.

General contractors, Plumbers, Electricians, Painters and more. All ready to start work. Except for the one problem preventing them from beginning work.

Damien and Maddison exited their car and stood in the middle of the street looking at the motionless contractors discussing a truce with a wall of several hundred people blocking their entrance to the home.

Damien walks across the street to meet with the general foreman who is

229

doing his best to calm the situation, with Maddison close behind; she stares out at the throng of people that have filled up the front yard. Her first thoughts are.

Where did these people come from and why are they here? She closes the gap and is now with her husband and Tom her hired contractor who is engaged with Damien and some woman claiming to be the groups spokesperson.

Reaching for Damiens' arm, she pulls him aside to question him.

"What is all this about Damien?"

"These people have all been helped from drinking the water and they are not accepting the house be renovated. They believe it is some sort of sacred place they want preserved."

"WHAT! Wait, No, Say that again."

"I am not repeating myself Maddie, come with me, so you and I can talk with them. The contractors can go home for a day, and we will settle this with them."

"Ok, I will tell the contractors to go home. This must work out Damien. It, had better work out or we need to buy another home."

"Maddison."

"What?"

"That may be the only option in this situation. I do not think they will accept a compromise."

Maddison slowly turns away from her husband, marching over to speak with Tom. Moments later the entire contractor teams retreated from the house as they paraded one truck after the other down the street and out of sight, back to their offices.

Now standing beside her husband, Maddison introduces herself to the woman leading the rebellion against her house and the renovations she had hoped to get finished so they could soon move in.

"Miss Williams may I ask you to disperse the lovely people you have gathered on my lawn. My husband and I would welcome a discussion with you inside at our kitchen table. I will layout our plans for the renovations and see if they are acceptable to you and the others behind you."

231

WATER

To their surprise the crowd begins to quietly disperse without a word being spoken from the elderly lady standing in front of Maddison and Damien. Damien ponders who she is and how she commanded the crowd without a single word of direction from her.

Damien watches the crowd clear the lawn eyeing each person then he sees the one man he never thought would be in attendance. Mr. Larson is in the crowd arm and arm with a woman. He looks extremely happy as the two walk away from the house.

Stunned at the sight. He questions.

Is this real, did the water actually help this man find a partner and the love he had been searching for?

Continuing a debate within himself, he contemplates, do we really need to change this house? Are we being tested?"

The lawn has cleared. Maddison is walking with her new friend into the house. Damien decides to take a moment to look around the house for any evidence this stand in was staged for a different reason. Walking around the house he finds there is nothing out of place. No indication of vandalism anywhere.

Damien decides to join his wife and her friend in the kitchen. Sitting down he decides to listen before he chimes in on the conversation that is being controlled by Maddison.

"Miss Williams, I agree with you on several points. This house has been a haven for many people seeking hope and cures from the "water," but my husband and I want to live here. This very house has been in my dreams since childhood.

The dreams started when I was old enough to understand what happened to my mother after giving birth to me. When I saw it I knew right away it was the one I wanted. I had to buy this house."

"Mrs. Steele your dreams are now the reality of being guided to this house. You are the chosen one to ensure it continues to help people. Do you not see this?"

Those words instantly changed Maddison. Her posture changes. She gets the same chill that has overcome her and goes away as quickly.

Damien is experiencing his wife in transformation. He cannot take his eyes off of her. He knows something is changing with her, but what is it?"

"I must leave you three to find it in yourselves to accept this place as it is. Changing it will change everything it stands for. You must leave it be."

With her last statement Maddison walks her out the front door and watches her walk along the stone walkway.

Damien follows out the front door behind the two women. He embraces his wife with both arms from behind her, both watching as Miss Williams avoids the mailbox just like Annette Lancefield.

Damien releases his arms from Maddison as she turns to look at him.

Maddison:

"You saw that, she does not like that mailbox. I have to understand what it is about the mailbox that makes those women avoid it.

Do you think I have been chosen to carry on the legacy of this house like she said? Is there truth to her statement regarding my dreams? Have I been guided this house by some power other than the "water? Please tell me I am not crazy."

"Absolutely not Maddison, you are not crazy, Although, she might be a little touched in the head. Especially when she mentioned three of us when she stood up to leave. I count two, you and me."

"Yes, she did mention three of us."

Maddison looked into Damiens eyes. She could not yet openly confirm to her husband what she suspected to be true. The blood tests drawn at the doctor's office have not been conclusive. But the home test did return a positive for being pregnant. She is still hoping the home test was inaccurate.

One big question remained on her mind. How did this woman know there were three in the kitchen and not just her and Damien?

WATER

Maddison reaches out for Damien with both arms wrapping tightly around him.

"Maddie, are you ok. Is there something bothering you? You do not typically hug me with this much intensity."

"I am scared "D" really scared right now."

"I understand. With everything happening this morning, it has been a wild ride for the both of us. Can we lock up and go home to my house and discuss our next move over some lunch?'

"Yes, let's do that. But I am not all that hungry at the moment."

"Now, I know something is wrong with you, when you do not want to eat."

"Soon, Damien, Soon."

"What does that mean, Maddison."

"Oh, Nothing my love. Go start the car. I will retrieve my purse from the kitchen and lock the door on my way out."

The two part each other in different directions. Damien to the car and

Maddison to the basement for another drink from the faucet.

Locking the front door, she walks the stones to the car but slows to divert her path away from the mailbox.

Maddison seats herself in the passenger seat. Damien waits to see if Madison says anything to him. She looks over to ask:

"Are we leaving or are we going to sit here?"

"I take it you failed to realize you've left your purse here in the car on the floorboard. Not in the kitchen as you mentioned earlier. Maddie I am beginning to worry about you."

Maddison surprisingly looks at the purse next to her feet, retrieves it, holds it up, then looks up at her purse to jokingly ask it a question.

"How'd you get in here? I swear, I left you in the kitchen."

Damien laughs it off, then puts the car in gear to drive home.

WATER

{1:30Pm Damiens home.}

"I Think I am going to have a beer with lunch. Do you care for one Maddison?"

"No, none for me."

Damien makes no comment to Maddison refusing alcohol. She does this often enough; it does not faze him when she opts out of his offer.

She knows too well if she is confirmed the choices she makes now, it could affect the outcome later. Damien steps out on the back porch to light the grill. Clutching her purse she informs "D" she is going into the bathroom to freshen up.

He is not paying attention to her as she slips off without him noticing. Maddison sits at the vanity. Envisioning what it would be like having his child. She has no mother to mentor her in childbearing and her father, the only person who sacrificed his personal life for her is now gone.

238

WATER

Looking back over her shoulder she reaches into her purse for another test kit. Silently she enters the toilet room and gently closes the door. A few minutes later she emerges, Not knowing whether to smile or cry she wraps it in some tissue and places the positive test back into her purse.

Damien has turned on the tv and is watching sports news, His favorite football team is heading into the playoffs this weekend. Looking around the room at his mancave décor. She wonders how he will adapt to her style of living when they do combine their households. They had been together long enough she should have thought about all of this before saying yes to marrying him.

Maddison walks out the back door; she smells the grill and becomes nauseous but holds herself firm and does not let it get to her. Stepping away so the smoke does not follow her. She begins a walk around the pool.

Damien takes diligent care of his place and of her. She admits to herself. He will make a good father to their child.

Her biggest concern at the moment is, will she survive bearing a child or will she succumb to the same fate as her

239

mother. She stops for a moment to wipe the tears from her face just in time for Damien to appear outside to check the grill temperature.

"Hey beautiful, I did not know you were out here."

"I know, you were too busy watching the sports report on your favorite team. So, I left you alone. Now thank me for being a good wife by preparing me a Caesar salad."

"It is ready for you. I did it while you were in the bathroom."

Maddison thinks to herself, does he know? How, what? Oh no he doesn't know, he has to be fishing." She places her hand on her lower belly hoping it has not begun to grow and shows signs that could not be ignored. I am safe for now. Brushing away that thought she walks to Damien standing at the grill placing his burger over the red coals.

The red meat and the smell of the smoke upset her stomach, she pivots hard and runs inside to the toilet, losing her cookies.

240

WATER

Above the noise of her vomiting, she can hear the toilet room door slowly open. From the corner of her eye, she can see Damiens shoes, "realizing" he had followed behind her.

"You want to discuss this now or should I keep pretending nothing has happened?"

With his statement he hands her a wash towel he retrieved from the hall closet on the way into the toilet. Maddison thanks him for his kindness as she rocks back on her feet. Knees still bent on the cold marble, her body facing the white porcelain seat always referred to as the throne.

Maddison can no longer keep the secret from him. It is too obvious and nothing she could say at this time will convince him otherwise.

"Damien, my love. Let me clean up and I will meet you in the kitchen shortly."

"Of course. I will wait for you there."

WATER

Damien walks out and closes the bathroom door. Maddison stands, turning the handle to allow for the rush of water to cleanse the bowl. She stands waiting for it to finish then walks to the sink. Turning on the chilly water, she splashes her face, reviving her red cheeks. The icy water soothes her face and swollen eyes.

She feels unwanted and rejected. Damien may not be happy with her being with his child. The moment of truth is upon her. She looks one more time at herself in the mirror admitting to herself. it is now or never.

Walking out, she finds Damien waiting for her. She slowly closes the gap between them. The room is silent. How to begin the conversation runs thru her mind. How do I explain to him her fear of having a child? This decision is draining her emotions.

Damien reaches out for her when she is close enough, engulfing her with his strong arms, She is comforted by the man she loves.

Maddison must now accept the outcome of what comes from telling him as she lays her head on his chest. His heartbeat is normal. Her man is not as disturbed as she figured he would be. A moment of silent closeness with him passes, when:

Damien whispers in Maddison's ear:

"His name will be Johnathan. We will call him John, John until he is old enough to tell us to stop. Then, he will be a man by the name of Johnathan."

Maddison uses every bit of strength in her to ask:

"What if it is a girl?"

"We will give her the name "Maddeline," It was your mothers' name. If I am correct."

"Yes it was."

"What comes to us, we will raise together. I will not let you die having our child."

"You may not have a choice."

WATER

Maddison breaks down in tears, crying with all she has to offer. Her husband and love of her life accepted her pregnancy. Without a word spoken from her.

He knew it all along.

WATER

A Noble Man

{10:00AM}

Damien slept in with Maddison as long as he could. With her sensitive stomach, He insisted she stay in bed to conserve her energy. Kissing his wife on the forehead he heads off to the new house to meet with the contractors.

A new direction has been considered between them. Given the recent standoff with the faithful followers of the house. Construction must wait until they can work out an appropriate course of action to preserve the integrity of the home and allow for upgraded renovations that would allow modernization.

WATER

Damien knew the contractor would not be happy with the delay in the start date and has come prepared to offer compensation for the delay to smooth things over with him.

Damien pulls up to the house. Tom is on the portico waiting on him. He does not look happy as Damien walks the stone walkway to greet him.

Damien now on the porch reaches out with his hand to greet Tom, who begins by handing Damien a bill and begins the conversation.

"What is this I hear you want to delay construction? Or maybe it halts altogether? This is my bill for the materials and labor for design work; I have invested in this project to this point. Are you willing to compensate me for this?"

"Look Tom. I know this is a setback for you as well it is for me and my wife. We wanted the renovations to begin as soon as possible but with the push-back we all witnessed yesterday Maddie, and myself need to reconsider renovating this particular house at this time.

247

WATER

You have to agree with us; there is something about the house and the "water." These people in the community do not want to part ways with. They feel if we change even the slightest part of this house, It will destroy what it stands for and its ability to heal the sick. Can you agree with that logic?"

"I do not agree with anything, and I especially do not agree with not being paid for my services invested up to this point. I will tear up the contract we have. If you are willing to pay me today. If you do renovate this house, you will need a different contractor."

"I will write you a check in full in consideration of a full release of contract. Do we have a deal?"

"Yes Mr. Steele we have a deal."

{11:30AM   Tom   leaves   the premises.}

WATER

Damien unlocks the door to enter the house. He begins thinking about last night's conversation with Maddison being pregnant and the renovations to this house after she was able to calm herself and finally eat a light dinner he prepared for her.

Walking from room to room his vision equaled Maddison's. This place is old; It needs upgrading in a bad way. Entering the room of photographs, he is taken back to the days of the people portrayed in every Kodachrome image.

Damien senses the room and the photos are different, then it registers with him. Every time he enters this "room" there are new pictures displayed, replacing the old photos previously viewed. There are so many fresh faces. The ones he knew were there, have been removed and replaced with a new exposure.

Damien's mind tries to comprehend how this is happening. Who is coming in here and changing the photos? He looks for evidence in the wall behind a few photos. If someone is changing the photo's then the pinholes from the nails must be changing. There is no way they are meticulously using the same pinhole for every photo in here.

Further investigating, he stands closer to one of the pictures to extract the evidence and conclude his investigation. A revelation comes to him. There is only one pinhole for each picture, and it has not been tampered with, only one hole exists for each photo. Not multiple holes as he was figuring.

He tries to remove a picture, but he cannot remove a single one from the wall. He moves to another wall to try again, then again on the opposite wall.

Abruptly he stops, looking at the exact position on the wall where a photo of the man in the military uniform used to be.

It has changed, "not removed," from its position. The photograph is now of someone else. Damien is confused as to why and how this could be. Thinking to himself, the photos are not like anything he has seen before. These photos are like looking in a mirror. Each image changes to a different person at contrasting times when he re-enters the room.

Then it comes to him, the reflections are from him, but not of him. Being in that room by himself, he is assuming the image of the person in the frame he looks directly into. It is the power of the spirit in the "room" reflecting who it wants him to see. He is experiencing the individual who visited the house in each frame. The room changes its reflection of him to become the person depicted in each frame.

The chilly wind Maddison experienced on several occasions inside the home now engulfs him. He is freezing as a short gust of wind pushes him back a couple steps.

He hears a voice and immediately the room becomes calm and quiet. The voice repeats. With a knock on the front door molding.

"Mr. Steel, are you in there?

Damien feels like a stone statue. He struggles to move; he is only allowed to speak out.

"Who is there?"

"It is Father Levi."

251

WATER

Immediately Damien is released and able to move. He rushes to the front door to get out of the house stopping suddenly only when he reaches the stone walkway. Leaving Father Levi standing on the porch wondering what happened.

"Please father forgive me for flying by you without greeting you, but I have experienced a revelation inside that house."

"My son you must be a noble man with morals and good ethics. What you are claiming does not happen to everyone. I am glad I stopped by to talk with you. Can we go inside to discuss your experience?"

"INSIDE? You want me to go back inside with you?"

"You have nothing to fear Mr. Steele. If you truly experienced a supernatural event and I will say, I agree, they do tend to shake people up. More the reason to reenter and confront it head on. Please, allow me to go in first. You will be protected. Then you can tell me what happened."

"Ok, Father, Is there something you need to do or say before I follow in behind you?"

"No, my son. You are not the first to experience the wall of photo's changing before you."

Damien walks in close in behind Father Levi. Entering the kitchen the two sit at the table and begin discussing his reasoning for stopping by. Damien asks:

"How did you know I had an experience with the wall of photos?"

"Mr. Steele let me tell you some history of this old house and why it is considered a sacred location to many.

You see since Annette's grandfather received the first photo and the many succeeding photos in the mailbox. Pinning them to the wall. He thought it would honor the people who had come seeking the healing power from the "water." Little did he know he would have more photos than he had wall space."

"I can see that now Father, But."

253

"Your question will be answered soon enough. When he passed away with his wife at the mailbox. His son returned to the house, walked into the room, and noticed all the pictures. He had never been in that room since he moved out.

The spirit in the room changed each photo, giving him the same experience."

"You mean they changed with him also?"

"Yes they did. This exact experience. So, the church elders have told me. This is not the first time the spirit has adjusted the photos and not the last time either."

"I am getting the impression Maddison, and I should "refrain" from making changes to this house."

"Annette was the first owner attempting to change the house structure. Her experienced was the same. Her involvement with the spirit that lives here moved her to sell the place to you. She simply could not handle it."

"That makes sense why she wanted to sell it at the price Maddie negotiated for it."

254

"Mr. Steele, I must return to the church. I hope our chat stays between us and whoever is in this house with you. Good day Mr. Steele."

"Thank you for stopping by Father. Would you mind saying a few words in the picture room before you exit? It would give me comfort if you could make peace with the spirit in there."

"I will see what I can do."

Damien is left at the kitchen table evaluating whether he should discuss this day with Maddison. He decides not to mention a word of this to her. She is already on edge thinking the worst will happen to her for deciding to carry the baby to full term.

He decides to leave the house. It is time to check on Maddie. Standing up from the table he knows the only two paths to leave the house are.

One, out the back door of the kitchen and the other is a path leading thru the room of pictures.

WATER

He chooses the path to the front door. The open framed entry to the picture room is in front of him. His eyes address the darker room beyond. Deciding on a plan he believes he can make it thru the room without looking directly at a single frame.

Assuming his chances are better if he looks down at the floor as he passes thru the door frame into the largest room in the house. The foyer is thru the next framed opening. His plan was effective; he makes it safely to the front door without incident.

A quick turn of the handle to open the door and he is outside on the porch. Keys extracted from his front pocket the door is now locked. A one hundred eighty-degree turn and a leap off the portico onto the hard stone walkway. With a few large steps and he is close to the mailbox where he abruptly "changes course" to avoid it.

The car starts easily and he is on his way home to his wife Maddison Steele.

Maddison is up; she has energy. To his amazement, Damien finds her cleaning the house. Over the roar of the vacuum cleaner, he shouts.

"It is good to see you out of bed and not leaning over the toilet."

Maddison sees Damien and turns off the machine while taking out ear plugs. She looks at her man and smiles.

"Did you say something my love?"

"I said, I love you with all of my heart."

"Ok, I thought; I heard something about a toilet."

"Oh! No, my darling you are mistaken."

The doorbell rings. Maddison informs Damien to get the door.

"I ordered pizza, I decided to give you the night off chef."

"You are such a woman."

Damien opens the door. A young man is outside the door with a large pizza in a box. He is slim and is shaking. Damien

257

inquires, thinking the younger man must be nervous.

"Are you all right? I have noticed you are shaking. Do you have a condition causing this or are you just nervous from delivering pizza to people's homes?"

"No sir, I do not have a contagious condition. No, you are not going to catch anything from me. The pizza is thirty-nine dollars."

Damien hands the boy forty-five dollars which includes his tip. The young man does not move after receiving the money. Confused Damien senses that the boy wants to say something, and he seems to struggle with asking a question.

"Is there something else on your mind young man?"

This triggers the boy to finally ask.

"Sir, are you and your wife the couple that bought the Lancefield home?"

WATER

"Yes we are. How did you know to ask?"

"Everyone knows who you are. As you can see I get nervous delivering pizza. Not only that, but I also get nervous doing just about anything. Do you think I can try the "water" and see if it helps me?"

Damien steps out of the house and shuts the door behind him to talk privately about the experience of the "water" and to inform the delivery boy it doesn't help everyone. Although he is welcome to meet him at noon tomorrow at the house to give it a try.

"You obviously know where the house is, so, no need to for me to write down the address for you."

"No sir you do not. I know where it is. Thank you, I will be there tomorrow."

Damien waits outside to make sure the young man gets safely on his way before bringing the pizza inside to share with Maddison.

Now inside he places the warm pizza box on the kitchen table. Maddison is smiling and hungry as she sits down and grabs a slice without waiting on Damien to get plates for them.

"Wow, I guess it's caveman style eating tonight."

"Hush, I haven't been eating regular for a week now. I am starving."

"I see that. Please do not let me stop you. You might bite my finger off."

"What took you so long to pay the delivery boy for the pizza?"

"Oh, nothing. He thinks he recognized me somewhere."

"You do have a cute face. Was he hitting on you my love? Did you inform him you were taken?"

"Oh! How you "jest" with me. I can prove my loyalty to women later if you agree tonight?"

"I just might be. Can't get me pregnant again anyway."

Damien almost loses a mouthful of pizza laughing at his wife. Finishing off the pizza they both lounge on the sofa with a movie playing on the TV."

{2:18AM Damien awakens.}

"Wake up Maddison. We fell asleep on the sofa. Come darling let's go to bed."

"I was more comfortable laying here on the sofa in your arms."

"Yea, well my arm is now numb.

WATER

The Reveal

{10:15AM The next day.}

Maddison is still lying in bed when Damien comes into the bedroom to entice his lovely wife to get herself up and dressed for her doctor's appointment. Procrastinating she rolls over while flipping the covers off of her. Damien stands at the foot of the bed while discovering his wife is full commando under the comforter that has now been tossed aside. She struggles that extra moment contemplating how to stand gracefully. Her back is strained and belly is showing signs of stretch marks.

She rubs her stomach and walks to the dressing room mirror. Gazing at her new form. Her hair is a mess. She has not been to the salon in a month. Maddison speaks softly under her breath, addressing her husband with only his name.

"Damien."

"Yes."

"Am I still attractive to you?"

"Maddison Graves Steele. If I ever say no to that question. There is a baseball bat in the closet. You are welcome to hit me with it to bring me back to my senses."

Maddison turns to embrace her man when he asks.

"Maddie."

"What "D?""

"Please get in the shower."

"Yessir, I guess three days in bed produces a different type of cologne huh?"

"Indeed, I will get the sheets in the washer."

"Are you going to the house again today? If you are, I will stop by after my doctor's appointment."

"I am planning to be there. I am meeting the movers at 1:00 pm so they know where to put our furniture."

265

WATER

"Why Damien Steele. You are finally agreeing to us moving into the house I love. Just the way it is without any of the renovations you and I wanted."

"You and I know that house and the people who have visited it will have our heads if we attempt to change to paint color. We have waited long enough. Everyone has calmed down and gone their separate ways. Even the spirits have left us alone. They, should leave us to ourselves now."

"Surely you do not believe we will never see another visitor and those spirits you've told me about."

"Father Levi said a few words to them the last time he was there. Hopefully, he convinced them to leave us alone."

"HA! You mean leave "you" alone, they have yet to bother me."

Maddison turns on the shower. The water flows from the shower head. It drowns out Damiens' last words he mumbles leaving the bedroom.

"Not, as of yet."

266

WATER

{1:00PM Movers arrive.}

Arriving at the same time Damien and the two men from "A couple guys and a truck moving company" greet at the sidewalk with a handshake. Damien leads the way up the lawn away from the mailbox then onto the stone walkway and onto the porch. Jorge' asks a few questions on when they should schedule the move from Damiens house and some items from Maddison's home.

Damien explains the details as he unlocks the front door.

"One thing, I would like to emphasize to you and your crew. No one is to go into the basement."

Jokingly Jorge' asks. "Is your watchdog down there?"

Damien turns to look him in the eye. Stopping them both in a face-to-face confrontation.

"No one is to go down there. "No one." Understood?"

"Yes, Mr. Steele. No one will go in the basement. Now where are the bedrooms and the living room?"

Damien finishes showing Jorge" the house. He and his partner finalize the move with Damien and are about to leave when Jorge' asks.

"I have one question before I go Mr. Steele."

"What can I answer you?"

"I cannot help but notice all the pictures in the living room. Who are those people?"

"People, who, I have never known personally, Although I now have a close connection to each of them."

"I will leave that alone for now Mr. Steele. Good day sir."

Maddison is parking her car as the two men start their work truck and leave. Maddison walks up the same path her husband takes, avoiding closeness to the mailbox. With a spring in her step, she bounces up the three steps to the porch and hugs her husband.

WATER

"Doctor said everything is ok. How do you like my blue dress?"

"You look fantastic."

"I like blue dresses "D.""

"I see this, would you like to go inside and discuss where you want the furniture set? What else did the doctor say about our child?"

"Damien."

"What darling?"

"My dress is a dark blue."

"Yes my love, it does fit you well. Now can we discuss the furniture?"

"Yes we can, We can go into the kitchen, and I can sit in front of you in my blue dress."

Damien is puzzled as to why Maddie is referencing her dress so much. They enter the kitchen where he pulls out a chair for her. Looking at her blue dress for something significant he might have missed. Sitting next to her he watches her form a huge smile. She also has lite blue eyeliner. He is trying to figure out this connection when it hits him. He jumps up

269

from his seat to shout as loud as he can. Then he picks up Maddison with both arms when she stands up to give her a congratulatory hug.

"IT'S A BOY!!!!!"

"Yes "D" it is a boy. A healthy boy."

After the celebration is minimized, the two finalize the furniture arrangement. Damien mentions.

"Honey, please go home now and rest. I will put stickers in the rooms for the movers so they know where each piece of furniture is to be placed then, I will be home to prepare dinner."

"Ok honey, see you back home soon."

Maddison has left the house. Damien is walking from room to room placing sticky notes with instructions for each piece of furniture. When he gets to the picture room he writes sofa on a yellow pad. Walking to the wall where he needs to place the note on the floor. He leans down to place the note.

WATER

Standing up he is shocked at the pictures on the wall in front of him. Quickly he turns to view the other pictures on the adjacent walls. They had all changed to the same face. His face.

The wall of pictures depicted a collage of his life, from birth, up to a young child, then onto his teenage years, then to his college days and finally to his present-day look. Everywhere he looked, every wall portrayed the same scenes. Turning in circles he had the same clips playing of his life.

He questions, how does this house, this room, these picture frames know "anything" about him but somehow knows "everything" about his life.

Standing in the middle of the room. Yellow pads in one hand and the pen still in the other.

The kaleidoscope of his life finishes. Now returning one by one to the faithful visitors usually shown. Little did he know he was given a lesson he would figure out why, later on his own.

Leaving the house, his mind could not stop pondering why the spirit has chosen him specifically. What is the caveat here? Continuing to drive home he passes

271

several blocks in a daze before he realizes he is almost back at his own house.

Parking the car in the garage he walks in to find Maddison. Once again he embraces her for an exceptionally long time. She assumes he has had another encounter and says nothing to him. Allowing him to hold her as long as he needs too.

They release, Maddison says.

"Come into the kitchen "D" and sit with me. Tell me what happened."

"I will start our dinner and tell you while I cook."

Damien prepares dinner for the two of them while he explains the experience after she left. Maddison knows not to try and offer her analysis or offer some explanation that may help him understand it all. It is for him and him alone to figure out why it happens to him, Especially when no one is near him or accompanying him while in that room.

These instances are personal. He can convey what happened all day long,

272

but she knows he has to figure this out on his own. Or he needs to confront the spirit head on and ask it why it has chosen him to interact with him. She suggests this to him.

"What do you think you should do?"

"I do not know Maddie."

"May I suggest you ask the spirit the next time it happens?"

"I doubt it will engage in a conversation with me."

"No, Damien, but you may get an indication in another form."

"True, but I do not know if I want to know Maddison."

"I think not knowing would be scary to me."

"Enough of this for tonight Maddison, let's eat dinner and go to bed."

"Wow! You do still love me, even with this pregnant body."

"You're such a woman."

"You're such a man."

WATER

{9:25AM The next morning.}

Damien silently slid out of bed leaving his wife still sleeping. Dresses himself then heads to his SUV.

While driving himself to the house. He decides he needs to know one way or the other, why did those pictures change before him. Showing him his life, changing slowly then rapidly then slowing again.

Were the pictures actually him or the son he was about to have. A fear for Maddison enters his mind when he realizes she was not shown in the changing pictures.

Was this his sign he was to be a single father? Did this have some meaning that Maddison was going to die giving birth to his son? He promised her, He would not let her die giving birth. But how can he prevent it from happening?

WATER

Maddison was right. He needs to ask. He needs to know.

Damien pulls the house key from his front pocket. Unlocking the door, he opens it and steps in the foyer, then closes the door behind him. Slowly he walks into the living room. Standing in the middle of the room surrounded by pictures of people. The pictures are not changing,

The silence is like nothing he has ever experienced. He feels his heart beating in his chest; The silence allows him to hear his blood flow in his veins. He can feel the spirit coming into the room.

It is time. He must ask:

"Why have you chosen me? I may not be the best servant for you or for the "WATER."

His heartbeat slows, he hears nothing. Once again the silence seems loud to him. Nothing happens. The pictures remain the same. Damien turns 360 degrees to view the entire room for changes.

WATER

Nothing is different or out of place. Stopping he contemplates leaving. Before he does he lowers his head, closes his eyes while joining his fingers together at arm's length in front of him.

His senses on alert. Listening, he hears nothing. finally, he decides to raise his head. While opening his eyes he sees. All of the pictures had changed to.

The Mailbox!

Bolting out of the house he leaps off the porch onto the stone walkway and runs to the mailbox. He stops, out of breath. Nervously he reaches for the mailboxes front latch then releases quickly without opening it.

Damien is not ready to receive what is inside. If anything "is" inside, behind the small door. Thinking back, he remembers being told the story of the couples perishing at this very mailbox. He does not wish to be the next one. Quickly he realizes he could rule that out because he is alone.

Now facing the mailbox, Damien reaches out again with his fingers to open the door of the mailbox. Hesitating he quickly releases the small, curved handle once again when he hears a voice.

WATER

"Good afternoon sir. Are you the new owner of this place?"

Startled, Damiens heart jumps and skips a beat. He had no idea the "mailman" had walked up beside him to place the mail in the box. He takes a step back while catching his breath, trying to calm himself before proceeding to introducing himself.

Damien reaches out for a gentleman's handshake.

"Yes I am. My wife and I recently purchased it from Miss Lancefield. Do you have some mail for me?"

"I do, but officially I must place it in the box. Then you can retrieve it. I must follow procedures Mr. Steele."

"Of course you do. I will step back out of your way."

The mail is now safely placed in the mailbox. Damien pauses before taking it out. Still miffed at why he was directed to come out here in the first place, he takes a moment to watch the mailman walk away

277

delivering more mail in the neighbors' box before turning his attention back to his.

Feeling safer about opening the front of the mailbox. He now opens it with his right hand while reaching in with his left to harvest the envelopes inside.

Sorting thru the stack he finds the normal utility bills that come monthly. He views the electric bill then his insurance bill, then a stack of promotional mailers and advertisements. Nothing is outside of the normal delivery. Again, he ponders the reason he had been directed to the mailbox in the first place.

Damien takes a step to walk away from the mailbox when the door opens by itself. He stops while holding the envelopes he pulled from the box, slightly turning his body while he turns his head to glance back at the mailbox with the door now fully open.

Damien frantically looks around his personal space for someone watching him or playing a joke on him. No one is near, no one in sight. He walks back to the open mailbox, "leans down" for a direct view to peek inside the now open box.

A hologram appears in the mailbox. It is playing a faint video of his life with

Maddison bearing his child in a hospital, then vanishes. He stands up. His mind wanders off, trying to attach the meaning of it to something that may happen.

Again, he leans into the open box as the hologram begins to play again. This time the hologram "reveals" his child "John John is a grown man standing on the stone walkway next to the mailbox. Maddison and himself are laying at the base of the mailbox.

His body thrusts backward, quickly standing upright, he stumbles backwards into the street behind him. Regaining his composure, he steps forward and slams the mailbox door closed.

Mumbling to himself.

"I have had enough of this mailbox spirit for today."

Damien, briskly walks back to the house, vigorously entering the front door and into the picture room where he openly declares.

"I am here to tell you; I have had enough of this. I stand before you a changed man. You have convinced me I

279

need to make changes to my life. If this is your way of showing me you exist.

Then you have succeeded. I now believe. What, I will not accept! And that is the ending you have shown me in the hologram. So, with that said, I have one request of you."

Immediately the pictures in the room turn to plain black and white. The faces have vanished; the silence returns to the room. The spirit wishes no one else to hear his request.

Damien takes the queue to make his request known to the spirit.

"My wife shall not perish giving birth to my son."

Damien waits for his answer. Just then the wall of once framed photographs that turned to black and white have now begun playing a hologram of the basement and of the faucet with the water flowing from it.

WATER

Damien takes this as his sign, departing to the basement he stands in front of the faucet. Miraculously the "water" begins to flow for him. Cupping his hands, he receives the water then raises it to his lips to drink it.

A cleansed feeling form within him. He leaves the confinement of the basement to enter the room of photos. They are back to normal. Including his favorite picture of the man in the military uniform.

Damien leaves the house, locking it up. He feels complete that he can now live in this house with Maddison and his son to be.

He has made "peace" with the resident spirit of the house.

The Mailbox

Damien traveled back to his house to inform Maddison of his encounter. He felt it was now time for them to move into the house without renovations. To be accepted they had to leave the place as it is. They will now raise their son to maturity together.

Maddison broke down in tears when she heard Damien describe how he negotiated with the spirit that she would survive child birthing.

"I should start packing our smaller personal items and the rest will need to be addressed by the movers. We will need to sell some of your furniture. We will not be able to fit both of our furnishings in the house."

"I see how this is going. It is my furniture we will be discarding."

"You know I love you. But this mancave stuff has to go now that I am the female in charge of décor."

"I love that about you."

"What part? The feminist strong woman who stands her ground or the loving wife that takes care of you?"

"No darling. It is the woman who lets me cook for her and the woman who knows what she wants."

"We make a good couple."

"Yes we do. Oh! one more thing."

"What is that my love?"

"Maddison you must avoid the mailbox at the house."

"I am planning on it."

{One month later.}

WATER

Now, fully moved in. Maddison decorates the house with her designer drapes and rugs. She tells Damien.

"You know "D" this house looks ok without any renovations to it. It is growing on me just the way it is."

"That makes me happy. I will be even happier when my son arrives. I plan on spoiling him while he grows into a man."

"He will be here in a couple months. You can spoil him all day changing his diaper."

"Ummmm what?"

{Johnathan Steele, "John John" arrives 7lbs 6 oz.}

As with newborns. Taking turns feeding and getting up at night became the responsibility of Damien. He loved his son so much, he instructed Maddison to leave the night duty to him.

WATER

One night John John was feverish with an uncontrolled cough. He was crying so much Damien was unable to comfort him. Walking around the house in pajamas embroidered with golf clubs and white golf balls, he entered the photo room.

John John stilled, he no longer cried and his cough stopped momentarily. Damien held him in his arms as John John raised his head to point at one of the pictures on the wall. It was of a young child his age being held by his father.

Damien peered at the photo and realized it was him and John John in the frame. Then the frame changed to the faucet downstairs. Damien knew the spirit was now directing him to go downstairs in the basement to get John John to the healing "water."

He wondered how this would work. It only flowed if someone was alone with the faucet. Damien had to obey the spirit. Venturing down in the basement with a feeding bottle he stood before the faucet.

While holding his son he removed the nipple from the bottle and held it under the faucet as the exact amount of "water" filled the bottle then stopped.

WATER

Damien held the bottle to John John's lips as he drank the bottle dry. The two of them now back upstairs in the photo room. Damien was pleased; his son had fallen asleep with his head resting on his father's shoulders.

Damien walked with John John's head on his shoulder for another hour before he felt the needing call for sleep himself. Entering John John's room. It was now time to lay him down in the crib. But before Damien could move him from his shoulder John John marked his pajamas with baby love.

{18 Years later. Johnathan is grown.}

The years of living in the Lancefield home never ceased to amaze them with the countless number of people arriving and sending photos of their success story.

New pictures and envelopes with donations inside never stopped showing up in the mailbox on a daily basis. Flowers continued to be dropped off at the footsteps of the Portico Cochere.

Maddison found Benjamin passed away at the mailbox one sunny day in the spring of the year, leaving the job of turning on the water to Johnathan.

{35 years later, at the mailbox.}

Maddison had avoided the mailbox for the number of years they lived at the house. Collecting the mail was always Damiens job. She was instructed to avoid it, and she always did at his request.

Except for this day. Damien was out of town playing in a golf tournament. He was expected back at any moment. Without thinking what could happen, she went to the mailbox to retrieve the mail.

It was a cold October day with a lite breeze. Donning a coat. Maddison walked out of the house, stopping briefly to take in the crisp fall air then took the three steps to the stone walkway.

WATER

Damien has returned from the golf tournament and parks the car at the curb. He steps out and sees Maddison walking out to greet him. She blows him a kiss; he watches her warm breath create a mist against the cool October air.

He walks towards her then frantically he realizes she is headed to the mailbox. Damien tries to yell out for her to stop. He is now under the control of the spirit of the mailbox. Refrained from making a sound, he is motionless, unable to move from his position.

All he can do is watch Maddison approach the mailbox, then fall at its base, lying motionless on the cold stones beneath it. Only then is he released from the spirit and rushes to her aid.

Kneeling down on the stone pathway next to his wife he picks her up in his arms, holding her tight next to him. With tears streaming from his face, he questions why, then falls to the spirit himself next to the mailbox with his wife still in his arms.

{One year later.}

WATER

Johnathan is standing on the porch looking out at the front yard, when a young woman appears from nowhere. He looks down and asks.

"Are you lost? How can I help you?"

"Are you the owner of this home?" She asks.

A simple "yes" is his reply.

"Then I am at the right place."

Johnathan replies.

"If you are seeking the "water?" You have come to the right place. Come inside with me."

WATER

WATER

About the Author

Michael Perry Allen has been an entrepreneur most of his adult life. Once an electrical contractor then a chef at his own restaurants. He is now retired to follow is latest passion of authoring fictional novels. These are the stories that have been embedded in his head for years.

Dedication

This novel as with my other novel. If it were not for my sister {Rebecca

292

Conaty Bruce} I would not have pursued my passion. It was her insistence that I begin authoring my stories.

Her novels can be purchased at

Amazon.com.

Irish Bones.

Esther Valentine chronicles.

Journey the healer.

Blueberry Wine.

Five spirits in the room.

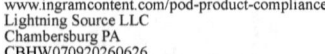